ARIADNE

Isadore Lhevinne

with a preface by David Miller

SPUYTEN DUYVIL

New York City

A Spuyten Duyvil Roots & Branches Series publication, derived from print editions in the public domain, copyedited for typos and any inaccuracies or discrepancies discovered therein.

Note: The author's unorthodox spelling of certain Russian names has been retained in this edition. We have also kept to his idiosyncratic language-use unless it seemed blatant that there had been a printing error involved, preferring to err on the side of latitude. In addition, we have not tried to suppress certain discriminatory expressions and views, which would have seemed far more acceptable at the time—to many, at least.

Library of Congress Control Number: 2023945254

THE SEARCH FOR ISADORE LHEVINNE

Isadore Lhevinne (1896-1935) is an enigmatic figure—a brilliant Jewish American modernist writer of the 1920s/30s who is so largely unknown that when I canvassed my fellow writers, none of them knew his work or even his name. Not that he was immensely well known in his lifetime—a somewhat (though not completely) isolated writer, he seems to have had no contact with the more significant and/or prominent modernist figures of the day, such as e e cummings, Marsden Hartley, Hart Crane, Waldo Frank, Jean Toomer or Kenneth Burke.[1] Also, until recently biographical information was extremely scarce, and there are still gaps in our knowledge of his life. For someone with such extraordinary talent, he's slipped into totally undeserved semi-oblivion.[2]

Of the people who do know Lhevinne's work—or at the least his name—I would hazard a guess that most are indebted to the advocacy of the US experimental film-maker Ken Jacobs; I certainly know that I am. I first came across Lhevinne in P Adams Sitney's fascinating book *Visionary Film*; in his discussion of Jacobs' film *The Sky Socialist* (1964-1968), which uses Lhevinne as a "character", he says that Lhevinne was "the author of two American novels, *Ariadne* (1928) and *Napoleons All* (1932), influenced by Symbolist prose."[3]

Lhevinne in fact published four novels—*Napoleons All* was followed by *Tsantsa* (1932) and *The Enchanted Jungle* (1933)—as well as a book of short fiction, *The Leper-Ship and Other Stories* (1926).[4] The allusion to Symbolist prose, however, is apt, if perhaps also a little misleading at the same time.

What Lhevinne is most concerned with is an exploration of states or forms of consciousness (dream, imagination, hallucination, vision) on the one hand, and a strong critical/satirical tendency (of both individuals and social groups) on the other. Also very apparent is his concern with music, both as a theme (composers and musicians abound in his writing) and as an ideal (both in relation to imagination and vision, and to writing itself in the way that words interact on the page in the realisation and, indeed, creation of imagination and vision).[5] *Ariadne*, his most experimental novel, is the epitome of such tendencies.

These are things that he does indeed share with the Russian Symbolists, perhaps Andrei Bely most of all, but at the same time his writing has its own intensity, tenor and texture. In fact, although he was aware of the Symbolists, it's hard to say whether he was directly influenced by them, as such, or whether he was working along parallel lines.[6] These same or similar concerns, very generally speaking, can also be found in some of the German Romantic writers,[7] for example, and then in much of German Expressionism (as well as such semi-Expressionist novels as Gustav Meyrink's *The Golem* (1915) and Hermann Hesse's *Steppenwolf* (1927)). If Lhevinne had an affinity with Symbolism, rather than an allegiance or an identification with it, that would bypass the idea that his work is belated and anachronistic, which I don't feel it is. Instead, he was indeed out of joint with his literary peers and, in fact, unknown to most of them. (*Ariadne* was most probably self-published, for one thing (as by Globus Press, NY.)) Too "wild" for the mainstream, not aligned with what there was of a literary avant-garde in the States, and too independent and strange and, yes, largely *invisible* to his fellow modernists, he was not destined for literary success.[8]

Although his work clearly had no influence, it's perhaps instructive to mention that works as disparate as William S Burroughs' earlier fiction (from the very late 1950s through the 1960s) and Clarice Lispector's *The Passion According to G H* (1964) have some affinity with regard to the exploration of extreme psychological states in conjunction with an experimental or exploratory approach to language.[9] This concentration on consciousness is not of course the only way we can approach writing, or that writers can approach their own writing: some may prefer the strictly textual, some more sociological/political perspectives (Lhevinne certainly had an interest in these), some more hermeneutical concerns, and so on.[10]

So who was Isidore Lhevinne?

He was born in Russia (Babruysk, now part of Belarus) in 1896 and grew up in Poland, moving back to Russia (Rostov-on-Don, then the Black Sea coast and later Moscow) as a young man, experiencing the Russian Civil War; he emigrated to the USA in 1920 when he was in his early twenties and eventually became an American citizen. He was a philologist and linguist, a teacher of languages, a musician and a graphic artist. His PhD thesis, *The Language of the Glossary Sangalensis 912 and Its Relationship to the Language of Other Latin Glossaries*, was published by the University of Pennsylvania Press in 1924. He travelled widely in Europe, as well as going to China, Cuba, Mexico and Ecuador. He died in 1935 aged 38 or possibly 39, of unknown causes.

What about *Ariadne*?

Lhevinne was prosecuted in 1929 over an obscenity charge against *Ariadne*, but the case was eventually dismissed. It is an erotic novel, but scarcely a pornographic one—if that's what's meant by obscenity. The distinction between eroticism and pornography is of course a well-established, possibly hoary one, but I believe apt in this case.[11]

The eroticism in *Ariadne* is part of Lhevinne's concern with the ecstatic, and is related to the hallucinatory, oneiric and epiphanic. But one needs to stress that this is conjoined with linguistic play, as well as offset by a critical/satirical perspective. These are the salient features of *Ariadne*.

Let us go to the question of *vision*.

It should not be forgotten that Lhevinne was Jewish and clearly very aware of his Jewishness—this is apparent from various articles he wrote and the periodicals he contributed to.

The author of *The Book of Joel* writes:

"And it shall come to pass afterward,
　　that I will pour out my spirit on all flesh;
your sons and your daughters shall prophesy,
　　your old men shall dream dreams,
　　and your young men shall see visions." [12]

Although Lhevinne's writing is not religious, at least in any conventional sense, "vision", in the sense of the awareness and/or making manifest of the spiritual (supra-material / trans-material / transcendent), is a term that can be considered relevant to *Ariadne*, but we have to emphasise that "vision" should not be equated, necessarily, with something of a visual nature. We can point, for example, to the importance of *oral* modes in various religious or spiritual traditions, as well as to the famous instance of God *speaking* out of the whirlwind in Judaism; we can point to the mystical significance of *the letters of the Hebrew alphabet* in Cabbalism; and so forth.[13] There *is* a strong visual or imagistic drive to Lhevinne's prose, but in conjunction with the linguistic in a very direct and intense way. He clearly had considerable skill as a writer, but his sensitivity to language doesn't exclude him using it with abandon at times. Vladi's more rhapsodic flights might give one pause, but I would venture that this is not so much a matter of any unevenness in Lhevinne's writing, as an indication of Vladi's immaturity before he passes through hellish and purgatorial experiences. Which may be the case with any of us.

With this edition of *Ariadne*, Isadore Lhevinne has come home.

David Miller
Bridport, Dorset

1   He did collaborate on two plays with Lowell Brentano, and corresponded with other writers, such as journalist Herman Bernstein, as well as publishing in various journals in addition to his book publications. The journals include *The American Hebrew, Jewish Tribune, The Forum, Literary Review of the New York Evening Post, Jewish Daily Forward, The National Jewish Monthly*, and others.

2 It needs to be said that Lhevinne is scarcely the only one to have slipped through the cracks of literary history: for a long time we knew very little about the Jewish American poet Alter Brody, for instance. Charles Reznikoff came close to the same fate as Lhevinne: only in late life did he begin to achieve more widespread recognition.

3 *Visionary Film*, NY: OUP, 2nd edition, 1979, p 364. Jacobs' film wasn't actually released into public distribution until 1988. I confess I have still to see it, although I have seen many of Jacobs' other films. For an in-depth discussion of the film, see David E James' chapter in *Optic Antics: The Cinema of Ken Jacobs*, ed Michele Pierson, David E James and Paul Arthur, NY: OUP, 2011. James also includes some interesting material on Lhevinne and his novels.

4 *The Enchanted Jungle* is a thinly fictionalised account of Lhevinne's own travels in Ecuador, with a (fictional) composer standing in for the author. It's the most straightforward of his novels, but I think David E James' characterisation of it as holding "little literary interest" (ibid, p 85) is peculiarly harsh.

The Enchanted Jungle was published by Coward-McCann in NY and includes a photograph of the author, showing him as tall, thin, balding, with glasses, and serious-looking.

Napoleons All, a very ambitious and accomplished novel, appeared from Mohawk Press in NY. It is centrally concerned with the Russian Civil War. *Tsantsa*, published by Brentano's in NY, is the only one of the novels I have not been able to see.

5 Does one really have to mention Arthur Schopenhauer here, especially with regard to music? Oh, come on: you all know this. Or can look it up.

6 In the article 'Proletarian Art', published in *The Forum*, vol 69, 1923, Lhevinne mentions Alexander Blok, Fyodor Sologub and Valery Brusov, but not Bely. It would be strange if he didn't at least know of Bely, however. Curiously, Lhevinne and Bely both included centaurs (!) in their writings, Lhevinne in *Ariadne* and Bely in his *Northern Symphony* (1904).

7 E T A Hoffmann, Achim von Arnim and Novalis would seem especially relevant here. (It's worth noting that Hoffmann was a composer as well as a writer, just as Lhevinne was a musician (violinist) as well as a writer.) Amongst English Romantics, the brilliant Thomas de Quincey stands out in this context. The Scottish writer James Hogg might also be mentioned—another especially brilliant prose writer.

8 For a relevant discussion of modernism and the avant-garde, see Matei Călinescu's *Five Faces of Modernity: Modernism, Avant-Garde, Decadence, Kitsch, Postmodernism*, NC: Durham University Press, 1987.

9 As a complete wild card, let me also mention Scottish writer David Menzies' *The Narcosis of Water,* published by Poetry Salzburg in 2017.

10 Doreen Maitre's *Creative Consciousness: The Metaphysics of Lived Experience and Its Relation to Literature,* London: Greenwich Exchange, 2021, is an excellent example of a study focusing on consciousness, although she has little interest in the more extreme states of consciousness. My own book *Art and Disclosure: Seven Essays,* Exeter: Stride Publications, 1998, might be seen as an example of the hermeneutical approach.

11 Incidentally, Lhevinne seems to have never been married, and we have no information about any romantic/sexual relationships he may have had.

12 *The Holy Bible*, Revised Standard Edition, NY & Glasgow: Collins, 1952, p 804. Vladi, the protagonist of *Ariadne*, is still young in terms of years at the end of the book, but he has also aged.

13   With regard to vision, compare the Expressionist Kasimir Edschmid: "They did not look. / They envisioned. / They did not photograph. / They had visions. / Instead of the rocket they created the perpetual state of excitement." (Quoted in Walter H Sokel's seminal book *The Writer in Extremis: Expressionism in Twentieth-Century German Literature,* NY: McGraw Hill, 1964, p 51.) See also *Music while drowning: German Expressionist Poems,* ed David Miller and Stephen Watts, London: Tate Publishing, 2003.

Vision and music might be something else to mention here: we have explicitly visionary composers such as Olivier Messiaen and (the much lesser-known) Dane Rudhyar: not the only ones, of course.

ARIADNE

Not long before the war, when the number of musicians invading New York was comparatively small—much smaller than the hosts that flocked here after the Armistice—there came to these shores a certain young man who, by his very temperament, seemed singularly unadapted for the strenuous life of a New York musician.

The young man's name was Vladi and he came from Moscow. He spoke little and never to the point. His was the silent eloquence of passionate grief; and he would wax sanguine over things meaningless to others. Now and then he would let himself be drawn into a reckless discussion, displaying a grotesquely exaggerated ego and a rather naïve conception of the practical side of American life,—the usual sort of romantic dreams, formless and warm. He even spoke with a certain dreaminess that was strangely irritating in a man who, at the age of twenty-five, had not accomplished anything as yet, and whose hair, furthermore, was visibly thinning. As he sat at the piano and played bits of César Franck's Symphony, he spoke, as if to himself alone, in his weird way about the trembling twilight star way down in the icy bottom of a lake: not a breeze to stir the wondering leaves, not a whiff to budge the rising fingers of the orphaned cypresses that are like a row of tin-soldiers awaiting other, warm fingers to tumble them down in a playful tussle. Like a song is the spectral magic of the sky, only there are no choir leaders, and no lovely choir boys to light the candles that will soon light themselves and take part in the heavenly junket.

Yasha Yashu, the gipsy, his only friend on board, said fervently:

"I understand you so well! It must be wonderful to steal horses on a distant star and run off for a week-end to another planet, and go places and see things . . . I understand you."

"And the souls of beings once so lovely, so throbbing, so warm, that hang on to the illusory edge of a cloud in the vain hope of reaching some place where cold may yet turn into warmth and where the ever-sought Maker may yet recognize their mettle and let them gambol anew!" He spoke softly and rhythmically as he played. "And now the cloudy raft passes by and the dumb despair in their eyes is answered by the steel glint in the lake. And night falls and envelops all, lake, bushes, clouds, and souls, and the silent drama merges with the opaque night."

Ladislas Lerner, who had heard the last words, remarked:

"Undoubtedly, this man will some day be a great— failure."

Ladislas Lerner was once upon a time a pupil of Rimski Korsakoff, probably no longer than a day or two, for he was ridiculously young. So consistently did he imitate the mannerisms of his late teacher that he almost succeeded in looking like a well-fed ghost of Beethoven. He did have a wistful gaze, however, and spoke dogmatically and trenchantly, not unlike a minor prophet.

Unlike so many prophecies, this one seemed dangerously true. Things went wrong the very moment he set his foot on Manhattan soil. Even the valuable letters from his teachers Auer and Glazounoff were of little avail, for he made one faux pas after another. He approached the wrong kind of people, charming but useless. And since he played five instruments equally well, his failures were quintuple.

One of his letters brought his trials to a sudden and peculiar end. It was addressed to a certain plutocratic widow, who had already been instrumental in creating several careers of magnitude, among them that of Ramsay Ventor, now Sir Ramsay, to whom she had taken a fancy. This woman of rather temperamental proclivities, an influential member of the Board of Directors of the Philharmonic, suddenly realized that her life would never be the same if Ramsay Ventor were not put in charge of the orchestra. Her life was spared, and Ramsay Ventor became the conductor. Unfortunately, his hair suddenly began to thin, and the temperamental patroness discovered that such decay in tonsorial equipment materially affected her susceptibilities. The man lost the conductorship, and the baton travelled from hand to hand, depending on various degrees of capillary splendor, until it landed in the sturdy hands of Toscanini; and so the female Mæcenas could gratify, at least vicariously, her hair-worship.

It was obvious that the woman who had spurned Sir Ramsay on such trifling grounds would hesitate to bestow the baton on an obscure young man whose appearance was not of a sufficiently high order to compensate for a possible lack of musicianship, and who had the extreme impudence of coming to pay homage with his head completely shaved! The hair-worshipper was both horrified and amused. Yet she was not entirely unimpressed by his hidden charm. She arranged for an audition; and since there were no vacancies among the violins, he joined the kettle-drummers. For he was in truth an excellent all-round musician, equally at home with the violin as with the traps.

He settled in the fifties and disappeared, seemingly forever, from the musical horizon. He knew very few people and very few people knew him. He had several pupils, but none of these held on long enough to him, because of his absent-mindedness and impatience. He was seldom seen in the customary haunts of Bohemia. He was not of the type that makes for intimacy. There was a nervous restlessness about him that precluded an attitude of self-sacrifice and abnegation which alone makes for perfect friendship. As if listening to some obscure voice he gazed above the interlocutor's shoulder, answered incoherently, and immediately apologized with a winsome Russian smile. But the harm had already been done—that of unmistakeably stressing his superiority. People do not as a rule forget such tactlessness.

Soon he no longer spoke even of his Symphony of Life. He seemed to realize that the very fact that he was a kettle-drummer — the lowest rung in the musical hierarchy—made such talk preposterous. Not infrequently people inquired with good-natured cruelty about the progress of his Symphony for two drums and a mouse-trap. In a fit of despondency he even resumed his violin studies with Miska Szabai, whom he fully for two weeks made gasp and call for a repeated rendition of this or that passage. Miska Szabai, the renegade, the greedy Hungarian Jew who spluttered and swore that he had never heard of Jews,—Miska, the favorite of the Tsars, offered to prepare him for concert work free of charge. He submitted to the strenuous routine for a while, then gave it up. Clearly, he lacked the mettle that went into the making of a virtuoso. He had strange visions of reincarnating the world's chaos in a profoundly stirring melody, the thematic development of which would purify mankind and relieve its tension. But his fingers stubbornly refused to tread in the beaten tracks of a chromatic scale.

Strangely sensitive to casual and remote resemblances,

he overlooked obvious analogies; resemblances that no one ever suspected and that everyone indignantly denied. He was actually drawn to Yasha Yashu because of a faint resemblance to a strolling acrobat's apprentice with whom he had been madly in love when a child. Yashu nodded in perfect understanding, twanging his guitar. He too knew the hypnotic charm of a casual resemblance, faint perfume, a sudden fragrance, or a quick smile that transforms a strange face into something poignantly dear.

They were not unhappy in their fashion. Through sheer insistency of Yashu, who thought it unwise to encourage his friend's solitudes, he was drawn into a lasting liaison with Neyla, a lovely model from a Broadway fur store. She had accidentally become Yashu's mistress; and when he left for a fortnight's engagement in Detroit, she switched to Vladi. Upon Yashu's return they alternated, surprisingly happy in their triangular arrangement. Neyla was of the type born into this world for love, just for love and nothing else. All she asked for her body and soul was mere appreciation of the noble magnanimity that was at the bottom of her acts. As Vladi was by his very temperament inclined to such an attitude, she felt a strange attachment forming in her heart.

Because he had seldom been seen with women, and because on those rare occasions the women were beautiful—obviously not his mistresses, since he was rather drab looking—it was assumed that his amorous activities had a trend toward a domain uninhabited by women. He was no longer an object of controversy. His career was dully complete. Only Yashu, the grotesque product of generations of unsurpassed horse-thieves, listened to his incongruous reminiscences and improvisations with a nostalgic smile. It was the sheer polarity of their natures that brought them together. Yet they had more in common than might be suspected, for they both viewed life as a musical revelation: Yashu as a comedy, Vladi as a pathetic song, a song in praise of a vision,—the one of whom he had dreamt all his life and whose vague contours he tremblingly sensed in the twilight smile of a casual mistress.

The strange incident, then, at one of Dr. Kreisel's intimate soirées not only upset all the notions about this obscure and taciturn man: it was the beginning of his notoriety as well. The stupefying event took place late in the evening, when all talents present, encouraged to the point of exhaustion, actually reached that point. Already Ladislas Lerner had played his mournful On the Ruins of the Temple, encored by the Song of Golles; already the fruitful discussion following close thereon had given rise to new inspirations and hastily jotted notes; already the cutlery and crystal ware in the adjacent room had sounded their reassuring taps and injected a note of almost boisterous vitality into the magnificent voice of Romauld Fishkin, who at the time was delivering himself of a martial aria: when the shrivelled Japanese shuffled in and respectfully whispered into the host's ear. And no sooner had Fishkin closed his mouth than Ariadne came in. Behind her trailed Count Rostovtsev.

Her eyes had the depth of sapphires. Like a sudden chord that completely transforms the tonalities of a quartette and reveals undreamt of backgrounds, her eyes fathomed the audience. Her appearance was like a sudden and refreshing change from brass to wood in a disquieting suite. Her almond-shaped eyes ran benevolently over the crowd as if caressing and inviting all and one to some strange festival, sealing the invitation with her dreamy smile and pearly teeth into which anything could be read.

Kreisel's soirée, dull as an exclusive funeral procession, at once began to simmer with pent-up curiosity. Beautiful women as a rule seldom visited the Kreisels, since Mrs. Kreisel herself was rather good-looking. It was murmured that Dr. Kreisel had been negotiating with the Count for an extensive concession in Russia, and was entertaining him on a large scale—avenging himself medically.

The unexpected arrival of Ariadne was of an almost

catastrophic nature. There was a preprandial lull in the air that is rarely conducive to any revelatory manifestations of the artistic nature. The program was over, and to save the situation, Kreisel vociferously announced the musical extravaganzas of Yasha Yashu.

Aside from his musical omnipotence, the most unusual thing about Yasha Yashu was the fact that his name actually was Yasha Yashu. Instead of taking to horse-thieving and thus satisfying the unappeased yearnings of his ancestors, he had espoused music, and fared just as well. The cosmic chaos to him was nothing but a musical extravaganza, and he interpreted it accordingly. If he only could, he would utilize the noises of blood pulsations musically. Powerless in this, he made good use of broomsticks and coins. He had been working steadily on the invention of an entirely new musical instrument that would embody the elements of all known instruments,—the glorious violaxophiano, a combination of violin-flute-piano-saxophone. Both hands and both feet plus the lips and elbows were involved in operating this one-man orchestra.

It was upon his musical shoulders that the problem of entertaining Ariadne suddenly rested. Out of his innumerable pockets he produced a gut string, tied it to two chairs, and suddenly shook the air with a tremulous rendition of Bach's Air. This was followed by a series of noises suddenly culminating in the March of the Sardar;

the performance winding up with an amazing exhibition of double-stopping whistling.

To all this Ariadne listened with her usual winsome smile, and it was difficult to gather whether she was pleased or bored. The Count, as beautiful in his male splendour as she was in her own, dropped now and then a word of approbation to Dr. Kreisel who, for the first time in the history of his soirées, definitely felt that the entire entertainment had nothing of the exclusiveness he and Mme. Kreisel had been trying to impart by dint of genuine black caviar, a butler, a valet, and occasional petty loans to struggling geniuses. Dullness is dullness, and not even the exotic extraction of Mme. Kreisel, who was a Lautrec—not the provincial De Lautrecs, but the old Normandy stock—could make up for it.

It was at this crucial moment that Yashu had the inspiration to command the magnificent and cold Ampico to play,—and to play a most unusual piece: the accompaniment to Mendelsohn's Concerto. Amidst the facetious protests of the indignant musicians he began to whistle the introductory bars, shrilly and ghoulishly. Ariadne began to laugh. The ice was broken. The evening was saved. A broad smile crept over the smooth face of Dr. Kreisel. With a sigh of relief he tilted in his chair. He never thought this daughter of an erstwhile army band-leader, who had never had the nerve to steal more than a hundred dollars from the regimental treasury, would be so hard to please.

But no sooner had the piano begun to drum out the Tutti, than Vladi slowly emerged in the center of the Studio, his eyes half closed, his face very pale. He took the violin, pinched the strings, and stared round him with a blank stare. His intentions were obvious. A burst of applause greeted him. The violinists were most vociferous, sure as they were of his downfall: they knew Vladi as a good pianist. The pianists, on the other hand, were visibly aroused, for they considered him a mediocre pianist and half-suspected a hidden violinistic talent.

As in a dream he gazed at the dark shadows round him. On the *causette* Ariadne sat, her nude arms gracefully swinging the fan. He loved her with all the intense madness of self-suggestion. The very moment she entered he had told himself that his life would hence be linked with hers; in what way it was not clear to him. Now he like a madman attacked the strings. The unsurpassed buoyancy of that unique concerto, the uninterrupted flow of its joys and sorrows stirred within him the pent-up grief of the years lived without her, years whose sole justification was that they led to this holy moment.

In the darkness her face bathed in a lucent limbo. He trembled and whispered her name again and again. There was magic in the very syllables that made up her name. It suggested dungeons and labyrinths and shaggy centaurs. As he conjured up these visions, his chest heaved spasmodically and a stifled sob welled in his throat. But he played on and on feverishly, until he reached the melodious Andante passage that relieved his tension, as if he had been playing for himself and not for her. The old Galiani sang in its rich mellow voice. It opened its soul to him, it had waited just for that evening to reveal the sweet mystery encased within its frail boards.

The last chords died away, the lights were on, but he stood near the dumb instrument, pale, oblivious of all but her dreamy eyes. "Excellent accompaniment," he mumbled, put the violin on the top of the piano, and clumsily walked back to his seat. Kreisel quickly emerged from behind and slipped his arm around his waist amiably, at a loss to classify this sort of berserker playing. To him, as to Mme. Kreisel, this unimpressive looking man had always been a strange problem, and at one time there had even been talk of diplomatically cutting him out of the soirée élite. Taciturn people, for one, would not be tolerated at Kreisel's gatherings. Somebody simply had to speak of achievement and potential fame. Vladi inevitably sought seclusion, and when coaxed into a performance, played strange pieces in an incomprehensible musical dialect. A definite ostracism, however, had been considered unwise at the time, in view of the surging vogue of futurism and the natural reserve which one was apt to feel in attacking a new and as yet not wholly interpreted movement.

Dr. Kreisel bent over him with the rounded smile of a man never wracked by doubt. His cosmic theories were simple and to the point: God created the world in six days and saw that it was incomplete, and so He created Kreisel. It was not even essential to ascertain whether the creation had been done in His image: the important point was that he, Kreisel, was cosmically drawn upon to fill in a heavenly lacuna. Yet he was not conceited; only now and then he pondered over the reasons for other men's existence.

"What a heavenly smile," he whispered to Vladi. "Notice her oval face, like a Giorgione Madonna with that wistful smile that seems to overshadow her entire being . . . By the way, I have the manuscript of your quartette. You forgot it here last time . . . I wonder . . . Mme. Kreisel is simply in love with your way of writing down music . . . You must autograph it and present it to her."

"Her smile is really strange," Vladi said, more to himself than to the whispering host, and his feverish words sounded like the introductory lines in Salome. "She is like a tone-poem, perhaps like Tod und Verklaerung. She fell like a meteor in our midst. Who is she?"

"Like a meteor, precisely, my dear boy," Dr. Kreisel

assented, fraternally slapping him on the knee. "She is the very symbol of perfect womanhood. Leave it to the Count. He knows what's what. Even her voice begs musical interpretation, don't you think so? It really reminds me of your quartette,—that second movement with its *Allegretto quasi fantastico*. One moment, Mr. Corngold, I think the manuscript is on the console table." . . .

"Do you know her well?" he asked, tugging at Kreisel to prevent him from a raid on the resting place of the quartette. "Who is she? I heard you call her Ariadne. Did you notice how long and graceful are her fingers, as if they were created to pry open flowers and dig into their sweet essence."

"Yes, she is worthy of being the mistress of a king," Kreisel remarked, cold with apprehension, for the first time aware of a definite system in Vladi's elusiveness. That young composer with all his earmarks of a genius—in spite of all possible borrowings from Paulsen and Monteverdi—was devilishly shrewd. The vision of the autographed quartette was now mockingly distant and yet more desirable than ever. He listened to the young man's vagaries, intensely admiring his strategy; and suddenly changed his tactics and said winsomely, almost coquettishly: "I must introduce you to her. She has already enquired about you. Your playing to-night was simply marvellous. It was really a stupendous sight, you, in the darkness, accompanied by a mechanical piano! She is thrilled, believe me . . . Suzuki," he suddenly turned to the butler, who was passing by, "in that console table you will find a music-manuscript. Bring it here immediately."

"Who is she?"

"She is the daughter of an army band-leader. It does not matter, does it? When a star has to be born, it simply is born, *c'est tout*. She comes from a small town from the Middle West. Strange, isn't it? Sounds prosaic, I know. Yet she knows how to handle those men from the State Department. They all dance at her bidding, like tamed bears."

"Doesn't she suggest to you the centaur tribe, a nymph in her own right, a lovely creature that came to visit men, her distant relatives?"

"How infinitely true," Kreisel exclaimed as the butler placed the manuscript in Vladi's hands. "Now, inscribe this, and let me cherish it as one of my priceless treasures," he added hypnotizingly. "Here . . . Right here. Anything you wish. Write. Here."

"You think she really . . . listened . . . when I played?" he asked with difficulty, and wrote: To Dr. Corngold from Vladi Kreisel. With a cry of stupefaction he noticed his mistake. "Let me correct it," he exclaimed, ready to cross out the meaningless inscription.

"No, no," Kreisel protested, delighted, seizing the

manuscript and rushing to Ariadne. "There you are, with your bewitching eyes," he cried out, triumphantly pointing to the page. "Look what you have done to a certain genius!"

She glanced at the page and smiled.

"The absent-mindedness of a true genius," she drawled. "I am intensely happy to know you, Vladi. By what right did this man deprive you of the pleasure of knowing us?"

"A most charming young man," Kreisel dropped busily. The Count bowed affably and ceded his place on the *causette* to Vladi. Kreisel diplomatically disappeared.

"How wonderfully you play," Ariadne said, extending her arm. He kissed her long fragrant fingers and let the arm drop. He did not know what to say. The melos of her voice enwrapped him. His sensitive ears caught overtones in the swift modulations of her voice that made him forget for a moment the exquisite lines of her oval face. It was almost unbelievable that she should speak to him. Was she not like one of those lovely silk handkerchiefs you can fold and tuck away in the hollow of your palm, then stretch out your fingers and lovingly unfurl the warm bit of silk not even crumpled? Curled on the *causette* like a pet snake, her grey eyes aslant with playful mischievousness yet full of cruelty—the eternal cruelty of the opposite sex—she suddenly drawled a few words in Russian that made his heart beat with faint

promise. Seized with an unearthly impatience, he quickly recalled and modified a passage in his Poem, with a sudden blissful smile realizing that it had all the elements of a truly inspired and spontaneous improvisation. The Poem was all about her, lithe and graceful like a Moment Musical, whom he had loved without ever having seen. It seemed that the years he had lived on earth had been but a prelude to that meeting, and the rest of his life would be a mere postlude, unavoidable as a coda in an old march.

He spoke with passionate eloquence about love, the shadowy substance of life—at least as real as life and as vague in its bliss. With all the delightful blunders of introspection, he listened to the music within him accompanied by her inimitable silence. Like two mirrors between which nothing has been placed and then reflected a million times with all the alluring details of a perfect void, their souls peered into each other. He spoke of a thousand things, and she read a thousand new things into them, as lovely. And, like an avalanche, their sudden encounter swept over them, and rolled into their hearts, and made them gaze into each other's eyes with flaming curiosity.

FLEET as the vision of Ariadne was, it seared his mind with its scorching breath. There was an element of mystery about her perfection. As if she had the supreme power of taboo, whatever she touched became holy and unmentionable. She came and disappeared like a falling star, without leaving the time to make a wish. There was not the slightest trace of her to give him the certainty that she had actually visited the earthly circle of Kreisel's Bohemians; but a morbid pang, a gnawing pain in his heart as soon as he evoked her image; not unlike the aftertaste of a disturbing dream impossible to recall.

She brought ecstatic dreams of greatness into his hitherto placid existence. Some day, like Berlioz, he might conduct his Symphony and see her in the box from the tail of his eye. Just what the outlines of the Symphony would be, he did not know; but his twitching fingers ran over the keyboard, and he muttered fragments of incoherent melodies that thronged in his mind. She stood out, pale, her arms stretched crosswise, as if crucified on the cross of cosmic harmony. Like a tempest the first movement swept along; like a candle she flickered amidst the raging whirlpool of sound. She was as living and real in absence as she was when he saw her.

Every day he sent flowers to her, inhaling their pathetic fragrance before sending them away to fade on her night-table. Outside of his creative work, he lived in a haze, hurrying through the numerous unnecessary details of everyday life; and yet it could not all and at once be sublimated into art, and whatever there remained in his soul of that love-madness was like a sweet poison. Whether he was slowly dying or being reincarnated, was not immediately clear to him.

Outside of the late hours when he bent over the five-line sheets, he lived and acted like an automaton. In the midst of interpreting a passage to a pupil, he would suddenly stop and gaze God knows where, or quickly run over to the desk and jot down a phrase. At such moments he was so intensely sincere, so absorbedly hearkening to a strange dictate that his appearance assumed all the earmarks of a second-rate actor trying to look natural. At other times he simply forgot a passage or a nuance. It was fatal. The voices he heard were discordantly out of harmony with what was going on round him. He gave up his violin completely. He detested it. It had held him in bondage and slowly sucked at his blood like an octopus. Where were all the fascinating sounds evoked at such stupendous price? A vague memory stirred within him, a pathetic face, a helpless smile, rapidly flickering by like all the lovely faces in the street-car, never to be seen again.

In his childhood he dreamt of becoming a great violinist and capturing the world or rather the woman that symbolized that world, otherwise drab and unnecessary. In the balmy air of a summer evening the tones he had evoked seemed to hover and vibrate long after the breath of them had fled. The days of childhood have a particular iron-soled step, and in between the day and night centuries are crammed. Yet he patiently stuffed his delicate mind with scales and came to love Kreutzer, and the arrogantly mounting, ever climbing scales. He revelled in their fathomless wisdom. The ingenuity one could display in combining the sounds was truly bewildering; one could ignore one note and let the other three leap or bounce, or smoothly blend two or three or nine or seventeen and dispose of the rest in as whimsical a fashion as one felt inclined.

As he grew up, the fear of falling short of the mathematical precision of each note became overwhelming. It was told of Miska Szabai that, in his youth, while playing for the first time before the Tsar Alexander III, he was so impressed by the Tsarina, that in the fever of inspiration he forgot the impish introductory passage of the last movement of Tschaikowski's Concerto. Three times he turned his flaming face to the conductor and had him start the *Tutti* over and again; then he calmed down and reached the cantilena and gave vent to all his unbridled passion. Soon after that he completely abandoned concert work and took to teaching.

In him, there was the same fear of spending the eternal stuff of life on fleeting combinations of sounds, however lovable, yet fragile and doomed like orchids torn from their native stem. A time came when he understood that life was but a variation on a minor scale. And with this understanding came also the complete loss of interest in purely violinistic achievement.

In time he developed a marvellous precision in reacting almost reflectively to the minor exigencies of life. He could eat, drink, speak, even teach, even respond to Neyla's fervid caresses, without being in the least able, at the close of each such function, to recall a single incident. Invisible, she guided all his actions. On the verge of crumbling down, his mind sought to conquer her, to evoke and hold her shadowy semblance until the wind should rise and blow it out. From beyond the dark window she came and bent over his shoulders, and gazed with a vague smile over the curlicues on the paper.

Across the street a Spanish violinist in a beret played with a pianist and shouted at the top of his lungs in exasperation. Of the two it was the violinist who never knew what is what, and Yashu even shouted once to them suggesting what was wrong. Yet they relieved the monotony of that street and fitted in so snugly in some of the extravagant developments of his Poem, the one that, like Berlioz's Symphony, was to subdue her. It was she who opened his eyes to the purely practical side of art. The self-sufficiency of art, so obvious to him before, was questioned now. So far, people had laughed at him. Because he was more or less chaste, he had the reputation of a pervert; because he did not visit the haunts of the dilettanti he was not even considered an artist; and because he seldom spoke of himself, people thought him conceited.

As he lived in a world created and inhabited by himself and his creations, all this was unimportant. The sudden vision of Ariadne brought him to the periphery. He had finished his Poem and the Prélude Symphonique, and he did not know what to do with them. Like all great and naïve minds, he thought that with the performance of these his quest would be at an end.

His first attempt to bring the Poem to the attention of the world was as unsuccessful as his first contact with the woman hair-worshipper. He took it to Ladislas Lerner, sometime the pupil of Rimski Korsakoff—for how long, his letterheads fail to state. Lerner belonged to that rather numerous group of Jew composers whose duty it is to serve as artistic windcups to the Jewish bourgeoisie. It is known that Jews are very sensitive to accusations of neglecting their geniuses; hence the actual neglect in which they hold their geniuses; hence also the vogue a few major nonentities enjoy, playing up to the very reaction such an attitude might bring about in a few more or less sensitive nouveaux-riches. Lerner wrote his own press notices, and syndicated articles about himself in the Anglo-Jewish press. One of these articles, Was Mozart a Jew? was even printed in a Canadian weekly. His literary achievements, together with his artistic appearance and natural shrewdness, induced yearly a group of matrons from the upper crust of the middle class to finance his self-exhibition under the caption of The Musical Soul of Israel. Now and then, to avoid accusations of self-perpetuation, he let another composer slip into his program. This, however, happened quite seldom.

He glanced over Vladi's manuscript and raised his voice to a loud hum. He admitted the conception of the poem was quite, quite interesting. Yet there was nothing Jewish about it. Now, he would not like to hear any jibes about the racial elements in music. It was true, he did not run an exhibition of synagogal music, but—he coolly droned on, anticipating a possible opposition— the beauty of purely Jewish music is supreme. There is a wistful haunting mysticism that like the yearning of an unappeased mind roams from desert to desert in the everlasting torment of an unconfessed soul. . . .

He forgot himself completely, speaking with the sweetness that invariably crept into his martyred Jewish voice when he spoke before the Ladies committee of the Anshei Chesed Congregation. Vladi's head drooped with weariness. He hated the man, and he hated the Poem, which now from the very contact with this mountebank had become musty and mildewy with bigotry. With a sudden hate he snatched the manuscript off the table.

"You talk just the way you play," he said breathing heavily. "Like a dinosaurus."

"It hurts to hear the truth," the pupil of Rimski Korsakoff remarked venomously, stung to the quick, for next to his compositions he valued his oratory most (except his face). "If you want me to be perfectly frank— let me tell you—your Poem is nothing but a rehash of Chausson."

"Chausson?" Vladi roared. "Anything but that. It's a deliberate lie. O God, why should you have said it? I am no competitor of yours, I do not write stinky Jewish music."

"Let me have the manuscript and I'll show you," Lerner said with as much dignity as he could muster under the circumstances. "No, I can't quote any definite passages now,"—it was obvious that he was very much aroused at Vladi's reference to Jewish music, for at the bottom of his heart he had dreamed of writing the great, national, Jewish Symphony, - even as every vaudeville actor dreams of playing Hamlet. "It is, I should say, indirectly influenced by Chausson in the very spirit of mysticism and the visionary limbo of the metaphysical aspect of . . ."

He slammed the door. All of his contacts with the outside world were like this. The completed Poem brought nothing but bitter disillusionment in its wake, and he was insane with agony, with fear, with apprehension. Days came, days went, and Ariadne was as far from him as ever, and soon there would come a day when she would disappear completely, Outwardly calm and submissive, but inwardly flaming, he rushed hither and thither like a caged panther. The great Max Eiler, the wonder violinist whose tone brought tears to the eyes of elderly women, refused to see him, even as he had refused to see anybody else ever since he became completely bald and could not draw a big audience. Yoakim Herst, the genius, just out of his *Wunderkind* years, could not be reached: closeted with his manager Lebenson, he was planning the final attack on Cecilia Carlstroem, whose phenomenal rise to glory threatened to eclipse even his own. The world was preoccupied with its own woes, and his Poem was not needed.

In a fit of despondency he went to Merrick Parrel who had been trying desperately to establish himself musically over the opposition of Herst and Eiler and some lesser celebrities. He had known Parrel when the latter's name was still Perelhoff and when he was still a *Wunderkind* and the most dangerous rival of Herst, both of them the greatest triumphs of the aging Auer. At the age of twelve he played before the Tsar and had the honour of kissing the Tsarina's hand. At the age of thirteen he had other women kiss his hands. When he was fourteen, the wife of an elderly banker taught him a minor perversion and attached him to her fading charms with the insane tenacity of a last passion. First love is sacred to men, for they love but once, if at all. He spanned the gap of thirty years between them with canine affection. After two years his face became virile, bewhiskered and hungry looking, no match to the cherubic looking features of Herst who at age sixteen still wore knee breeches and was headlined as the ten-year-old Paganini of the twentieth century. In America too the public somehow did not take to Parrel where it worshipped Yoakim Herst. The affection of the St. Petersburg banker's wife hung over him like a curse.

He recognized Vladi with a grouchy nod of his pale face and rubbed his unshaved square jaw with his immensely long and bony fingers.

"What do you want me to do?" he asked.

"Parrel, I want you to play this Poem at the forthcoming Wolheim Prize competition," Vladi said, unfolding the manuscript.

"I don't want any modern stuff," Parrel snickered. "I am playing Bach's Chaconne."

Vladi looked into his eyes. There was a lifelong agony in their moist sheen, a tragic bewilderment at the incomprehensible panorama of life. He wanted no modern music! The very word modern seemed to make him froth at the mouth. He was afraid of life, and, like an ostrich, dug his face away from the turbulence that led nowhere. Perhaps the word suggested the elderly wife of the banker.

"I don't want any modern stuff," Parrel hammered distinctly, looking at Vladi with elemental hatred, as if he saw in him the cause of cosmic evil. "I'll throw in some Kreisler or Weniawski for good measure. I shall not exert myself. The prize is as good as mine," he added with a haughty smile, wringing his fingers. His wrist was long and hairy, and it was said that there was not a combination of sounds that his long hand could not elicit from the violin. The fingers were thin and greedy, like his eyes, like the once sensuous mouth, now thin and discolored. "You know how little I think of such prizes."

"My life depends on it," Vladi said. "Parrel, we had the same master once upon a time, we played the same things, we followed the same instructions and dreamed the same dreams. These are all embodied in this Poem."

"Dreams come and go."

"Yet some dreams linger forever."

"Yes, bad dreams."

"Even bad dreams are sweet after they have been dreamt," Vladi exclaimed with abandon. "I would dedicate this Poem to you, if it were not Ariadne's by right. . . . God, how I love her! The very rustle of her dress sets my blood seething. I have been cursed with love, and I can love no one but her. This is my only chance, Parrel. Who am I to set my eyes on her whose very voice is perfection?"

He moved his chair closer to Parrel and touched his angular elbow with deep affection. Parrel shivered and stared at him with amazement.

"It doesn't matter," he at length said, "I can't learn it by heart."

"You can prepare it in one week with your colossal memory," Vladi cried out, sensing a faint note of irresoluteness in Parrel's screechy voice. "Listen to this passage. . . . Is this your Strad?"

He tuned the violin, one of the three Strads worth at least one beautiful human life; the price the banker's wife paid for Parrel's fall. "There is nothing to it," he murmured. "It flows like an inspired improvisation. Just listen—just strike those few chords, Parrel, as you used to do, with your wonderful pianistic hands."

He played the Poem in high fever, and Parrel struck not only the introductory chords but followed him until the last chords merged with the air and there was again the silence of a drab afternoon.

"I can't play it," Parrel suddenly said, wiping his forehead. "Don't try to convince me, Corngold. And don't stay here too long, I am expecting my mistress. I am sleeping with her to-day." And he added an obscene word and laughed loudly and vulgarly, then sank in his chair and sighed. "Ah, you are a nut, Corngold. This isn't the way to get women. Suppose I do play it. You won't get her. All you want is to sleep with a woman. Don't talk to me about her soul. The easier you get her the less you know about her soul. . ."

Again he swore and chafed and reveled in short obscene words. His fingers twitched nervously as if seeking substance in the very air to rend into shreds and scatter to the winds. There was an ancient hunger in his narrowed eyes that instilled a cold fear in Vladi's heart. He rose and quietly gathered the scattered sheets of the Poem.

"Why don't *you* compete?" Parrel asked lingeringly. "You play—well, you play rather decently. Better than Anisov, or his brother De Castro. Much better. Isn't it queer how Jews fall for such cheap names—as if Rosenberg were not good enough?"

Without saying a word Vladi slammed the door behind him.

WITH an unexpected doggedness he peddled his Poem, grateful to Providence that his orchestral duties laid no claim on his time. Drumming as a profession may not be exactly recherché, yet it marvellously fits in with certain artistic temperaments, especially those inclined to meditative indolence. True, there are invariably difficulties in conveying just the proper impression as to one's importance. One has to battle against a cold world securely entrenched behind its own valuations. Yashu himself had considerable difficulties in introducing him to the exclusive musical soirées of Dr. Kreisel, himself a poet, musician, painter, real estate dealer and performer of illegal and profitable operations. Mrs. Kreisel had to acquiesce, for Yashu's own resourcefulness was so indispensable that he had to be humored. Vladi, after all, paid in usual currency for the caviar consumed at the gatherings. He played excerpts from his quartette, and Mrs. Kreisel liked them, especially "all those passages that are so, so reminiscent of Ravel and Paulsen, a rather obscure Dutch composer of the XVII century." Vladi scarcely noticed the pungency of her remark, unimpressed as he was by anything people said. Two weeks later the entire quartette was performed in the Studio, and again—this time Dr. Kreisel himself—spoke of lovely reminiscences from Monteverdi.

Night after night he had worked on the Prélude

Symphonique and the Poem, in hope that Dr. Kreisel, who boasted of newspaper connections and of a lasting friendship with James Huneker, would help him. He was entering a new phase of life: he became cognizant of the outside world, a dream within a dream. His eyes red and his mouth dry from too much smoking, he paced his room nervously and hummed and wrote on the go. Sometimes, toward dawn, he would get up and, walking as if in a trance, reach the manuscript and cross out several bars and hastily jot down a new passage. Once he actually dreamt of writing the Andantino movement: he saw himself sitting on the shore of a mountain lake, listening to a sustained voice rolling over his shoulders. With bated breath he took the heavenly dictation. It was but a dream, and he woke up suddenly with a strange ache in his heart. The woman behind him could not be seen, but he recognized her voice in the miraculous harmonies she had conjured out of the cliffs. Folding his hands, staring into the grey nascent dawn, he murmured her name as if he were never to see her again. It was thus that the Andantino was written.

He played both things to Yashu and to Feofani, an ugly Russian of Greek origin, whose very ugliness had once made him sensationally successful both with women and in art. For a short while, years back, Vladi had been his pupil, then instructor in his Conservatory in the South of Russia. Weary, downcast, disgusted with his drab life in America, Feofani was happy to drop in and borrow a few dollars and have a drink or two. Yashu, who considered all men from the standpoint of a cannibal, had an eye on the histrionic possibilities of his ugliness, and even suggested blandly that Feofani was ugly enough to join him in the exploitation of his now ready violaxophiano. Feofani smiled contemptuously. His fat lips drooped and his low forehead became pleated. He thought eternally of his four beautiful wives and the strange ways of money. He loved and understood women, and they had loved him for his love. He loved and understood music and could speak entrancingly of it with a fire that cast a spiritual beauty over his grotesque face; yet life itself was so much more bewitching than any art, however perfect.

"Take it to Miska Szabai," he suddenly said to Vladi with a strange grimace that made him look like a caricature of Miska. "I know him well. I am sure he could induce Eiler to play it. It's no use, Vladi: both things you have written are masterpieces. I say so."

"Miska Szabai would not speak to me," Vladi retorted. "He is busy now getting married to his housekeeper."

"A great artist with all his foibles," Feofani sighed. A dreamy smile hovered over his lips, and it was difficult to ascertain whether he referred to the great genius of the teacher of seventeen geniuses, or to the sexual potency of the thick-lipped Hungarian Jew who had been in the habit of seducing most of his pupils, and who now at the age of eighty married a woman at least twenty years his junior.

"No, there isn't much money in composing," Yashu, the potential horse-thief, commented. "It's a pity the Prélude Symphonique is too good for my violaxophiano. It would go over the heads of American idiots."

"It would go over the heads of any idiots," Feofani said. "A rose is a rose, and garlic is garlic. But what should we make out of, say, carburetium nastolicum? Who knows what it is? Write a sensationally sentimental ballad and the world will bow before your greatness. A man who is equally at home with piano, violin, oboe, flute, and drums should be the conductor of the Philharmonic— or a barber."

"No, it is wonderful to be honest to oneself," Vladi said, and in the growing dusk his voice had an almost prophetic touch. "To return the precious fire unsullied to the eternal Maker!"

"And if there is no Maker?" Feofani jeered.

"It's immaterial. There is an eternal source of life to which everything returns after the allotted span of seconds. Somewhere that torch flickers and casts a fantastic gleam over heavenly hills and dales, and divine harmonies resound there, and their echo reaches us here on earth, and in vain do we try to recapture their untranslatable strains."

"Sounds like Lermontov," Feofani said, with a quiver. He felt Vladi's breath, and it seemed to him for a fraction of a second that it was the breath of some Supreme Being filling the darkness of the room.

"Lermontov or Plato, but our hearts are wrung with a strange ache, and we cry to our inner heaven. All my life I have been striving to express just what was stirring in my heart."

"No, there isn't much money in composing," Yashu repeated. "However, you needn't worry, Vladi. I'm leaving on a tour with my one-man orchestra, and there'll be enough money in it for all of us."

"Such money is unworthy of a true musician," Feofani said sarcastically. The very word violaxophiano made him see red, because it was the symbol of a prosaic country, a country that knew no demarcation line between art and circus, emotion and stunts. That gipsy, who would have never dared approach him in Russia so familiarly, stirred with a sudden witchcraft the days of not so long ago, and his slow progress downhill.

"God, O God, I shouldn't have played baccarat on that fatal night," he groaned, "and I wouldn't have lost fifty thousand dollars—and I wouldn't be here. Oh, how sweet, how lovely are the nights in Rostov, and what beloved vistas the faint breeze from Northern Caucasus raises in your soul!"

Vladi quickly turned to the last movement of his Prélude, asking advice, to tide Feofani over his confessional mood. They all knew that he had fled Russia because he had played heavily, lost the school funds and pretended to have been held up. His fourth wife had just died—a beatific girl with golden hair and the translucence of a truly beautiful consumptive—and he somehow felt tired and unable to summon enough conviction into his voice. It was so immaterial to him whether they would believe him or not—and they did not.

Yashu brought in a bottle of Martel, and Feofani calmed for a while. After several drinks he spoke about his old triumphs, though he knew that they knew he was a liar, and that as a violinist he never amounted to much; that he owed his administrative successes first to an uncle, who was a court favourite, and then to his brilliant witticisms, salacious anecdotes, and profound culture. Now he spoke of Thomson's Passacaglia, and because it suddenly evoked in his mind the difficulties he could never surmount and how these had led to his acquaintance with his first wife, a brilliant violinist, his voice became dangerously trepidating. His hands quivered, his entire being became shrivelled, as if he only now realized the inexorable course of eternity.

He rose and laid his hand on Vladi's shoulder with

dumb despair,—and his stooped back was as pathetic as an elderly aunt dancing with her niece at a charity bazaar.

A FEW days later Feofani came and declared that the great Kazarinoff had consented to examine the Prélude Symphonique.

"Kazarinoff!" Vladi repeated, fascinated. "Do you remember, Feofani, how I played before him,—the seven of us, instructors in your Conservatory? He sat in the corner like a shadow, and we were burning with true inspiration."

"Have you the manuscript ready?" Feofani inquired in a business-like tone. With a sudden pang in his heart, with a mocking clarity he saw all the unforgettable details of that evening. It was just a month after he had met his third and loveliest wife. It was strange how cruelly the present was rooted in the past and how heartrendingly it mapped the future. Because his life had already been lived, because he felt an overwhelming tiredness at the remote possibility of a fifth wife, he, like a maniac, sought oblivion in the sweet bitterness of a colorful past.

"I remember that lovely hall, where you once played that Borodin quartette, where that divine Nocturne occurs," Vladi reminisced with abandon, pouring the drinks. "And Kazarinoff sat and listened to you, and then your wife, like a white vision. . . ."

"Let's go," Feofani huskily said, wiping his fat lips.

Outside it was raining. The persistent patter of the oblique rain wove its martial rhythms. Feofani drummed the keys with his chubby fingers. He was the bearer of four beautiful lives and their immortalities, and with his rapid slide downward their beatific souls shrank and shrivelled—Eulalia, Xenia, Aglaya, and Lola. The efforts he had made of late to stand up and lift their sagging souls into the immaculate azure of nonexistence had become less and less effective. Their very features were now dimmed, and he clung to Vladi as to a miraculously found link with a past that by now had acquired all the reality of a dream. He even discovered a disturbing resemblance between Ariadne and Aglaya, the one he had loved most, the one he had lost in a most bewildering fashion. And so every day, as soon as he was through with the Capitol, where he played the viola, he dropped in to see Vladi and have a drink or two. He clung to him with the faith of a Moslem pilgrim, craving the sole privilege of basking in the other man's genius and dreading to merge with the grey mass around him. In art, eternal, imperishable, he sought the missing soft lining for his four wives' coffins.

They walked to Kazarinoff's studio in the seventies. It was still raining. Red and green lights shone in the soft dampness of the streets like tears in the sunshine.

They found Kazarinoff in his huge studio, cold and empty but for two Steinways, lacquered monsters squatting on their hind legs, their ivory maws ready to snap. Vladi calmly put the manuscript on one of the grands. Kazarinoff glanced at it, his shoulders stooped and hostile, his yellow Tartar face all screwed up in an effort to ridicule the potential genius. He had seen thousands come and go and never come again.

"This is a Prélude Symphonique for piano and small orchestra," he said in a voice drab and dull from lack of practice.

"I shall supply the orchestral accompaniment," Vladi said. "I think I remember most of it. I love it too much. I dream of it. I live on it. It's the best thing I ever wrote."

"It is," Kazarinoff dully repeated, wrinkling his browless forehead.

"Ah, ces componistes!" Feofani exclaimed, in vain trying to veil his excitement with ironic bon-mots. Again he was in the presence of his childhood friend, at whose feet he now wanted to throw himself and worship and forget himself in his evocation of Aglaya, whose courtship was concurrent with his loveliest associations with Kazarinoff. The town of Rostov was in bloom then, the air was laden with heavy scent of jessamine, and Aglaya, like an odalisk, sat at his feet drinking in the depths of his wisdom. At night, after ten hours of practice, Kazarinoff would slip into the empty hall of the Conservatory, and there they would play César Franck's or Beethoven's Sonatas, and reminisce of their days in St. Petersburg and their common friends Chaliapin, Auer, Glier and a host of others. Perhaps it was these titanic associations more than anything else that made Aglaya love him. And now, into Vladi's passionate outbursts he read his four loves, complete like an electric circuit and as benumbing.

"Proceed then," Kazarinoff said sternly, and Vladi started the orchestral introduction. He stared at the tragically huddled behemoth-looking Feofani, whose triangular radish-like head suddenly shrank into his shoulders and drove the entire body out of the room into the rainy night. Seized with a burning pity, he felt that his strength was forsaking him, that his hands began to quiver under the impact of all the shadows that now beleaguered his mind and begged reincarnation. Above all towered the drunkenly swollen face of Moussorgski, his hairy chest bare, his face besotted and bleary; yet so gleaming were the eyes that Vladi moaned and suddenly attacked the keys with frenzy and shouted:

"Now!"

Kazarinoff, stupefied, touched the keys with his unsurpassed gentleness, and a majestic melody resounded in the cold hall. The orchestral accompaniment tore into the melody and there was a dynamic clash between the stubbornly unyielding pathos of the ever recurring tune and the perpetual inventiveness of the variations. As if a tempest had risen, as if a whirlpool had engulfed both the music and the creators, the sounds cried to heaven and the walls received them with cold acquiescence, and the very ceiling seemed lower as if straining its white ears to take in the precious melodies that flew from beneath his fingers.

But when they reached the last two pages, where all the challenge had spent itself and given way to resignation without the slightest intimation of potency, and the piano sang its swan song, Vladi suddenly dropped his arms and stared vacantly at Kazarinoff.

"Go on! Go on!" the pianist shouted. "Finish it!"

"I can't!" Vladi cried. "I can't. It's above me."

"What's the matter with you?" Feofani asked, aroused from his strange reveries. He had just dreamt he had won a hundred thousand dollars in baccarat and rehabilitated himself completely—and suddenly discovered that it was all useless, since his four wives were dead.

Vladi quickly rose and turned aside, weeping helplessly.

"Forgive me," he stuttered. "I couldn't help it. When I wrote it, I wept. And whenever I play it, tears flood my eyes. It is dedicated to Moussorgski, and this is the least I can do to honour the memory of that great spirit."

He wiped his eyes, but his chest was heaving convulsively and he bit his lip to check the nasty trembling of his jaws.

"Very, very emotional," Feofani whispered, shaking his big head. "Well, what do you sat, Serge?"

Kazarinoff's thin parchment-skinned fingers ran

over the keys in quick feverish reminiscences of the pathetically unexpected tribute to Moussorgski. Unconsciously he turned to the manuscript and continued playing from the pages. The ecstatic litany quivered in the avid spaces of the hall like an agonizing voice in the mountains. Kazarinoff's face glowed with the pallor of inspiration: he recalled his friend Borodin who had spoken to him of Moussorgski. His eyes kindled with anguish, and suddenly he raised his hand aloft and shouted: Now! . . . Vladi ushered the triumphant *Tutti*, and thus they entwined their memories and woes into the musical network until the last chord resounded and died on the trembling panes.

Kazarinoff lifted his deep set eyes, looked coldly at Vladi, and said in his usual dull voice:

"Good. Leave the manuscript here. I shall play it."

In the street only, he realized that the man with whom he had spent an hour was Kazarinoff. He spoke endlessly, sprawling all over the sidewalk, and sliding like a child. On the corner of Sixtieth Street he fell in the gutter, dragging Feofani into a puddle. He laughed with a naïve helplessness and cleaned Feofani's coat. He wanted to speak about Ariadne, the beloved being whose very attributes were unmentionable like those of the God of the cabbalists. She winked to him amidst the fantastic play of lights. As if to strain her receding vision to his chest, he flung his coat open and burst into wild oratory. It was on a night like this that he and six other violinists played Kazarinoff's *One Lonely Voice*, a haunting *vocalise.* Beautiful moments must recur. There was a deep mystery about life, and now even the complete disappearance of all being did not seem so torturous. There was a significance in all, being and not-being. He recalled the effeminate smile of Aglaya, who adored musicians and basked in their warm harmonies like a nymph. Her smile was still living and inviting in its warm moistness. In spite of her death she persisted in her lovely outlines.

And now her unearthly loveliness breathed a calm reassuring message in the damp chaos of the February night, even as an opalescent star murmurs to the uncertain wanderer.

There remain but a few incidents to be told here before the final appearance of Ariadne and the beginning of Vladi's strange dreams and quest of her. He came face to face with her at the rehearsal of the Prélude Symphonique, under rather unusual circumstances, even as he had dreamt of meeting her. For there are moments in the life of every artist when even the wildest dreams come true for a while—even if they do not lead to the culmination that makes the dream so disturbingly beautiful. Undoubtedly, the sudden recognition accorded him by the great Kazarinoff had wrought a profound change in his very dreams of Ariadne. Also, in the erratic behavior of Parrel he sensed the potential power of the Poem. After he had become famous overnight, he could approach her as his equal.

The days between his first meeting with Kazarinoff and the rehearsal were filled with unforgettable reveries. In the evening he lay in his bed enshrouded by the dusk that slowly crept into the room, listening to the muffled tones of the pianist across the street now gorging himself to his heart's content in the absence of the bereted and dyspeptic violinist. Twilight tickled his eyes gummed with warm tears of a stirring anticipation. Something momentous was about to happen. He was like a woman expecting a child. The vanishing chords of some popular insipidity blended with the poignant sinuousness of a half-forgotten Andantino from Mozart or Schubert. Against the unreal background of the vanishing strains it required no effort to reconstruct the dream of Ariadne. Those whom he had seen a hundred times were almost as real as she whom he had seen but once.

As unexpected as all she did was her sudden appearance in the Aeolian Hall. Dark, cold, and hostile during the day, it was like a morgue remaining for a while without corpses to give it the aspect of inhabited quarters. A few artistic heads were sprinkled here and there amidst the deserted tiers of the chairs. Max Eiler's completely bald head shone with malicious

conspicuousness next to the purple nose of Abraham
Eiler, the real-estate magnate and former Russian
barkeep. More or less obscure but promising looking
makes and females added to the general drabness. A
determined woman with an expression of deathly finality
on her square face fussed about the stage announcing
the names and qualifications of those deemed worthy to
take part in the final round of the five-thousand-dollar
Wolheim prize. Just then a ludicrously fat Jewish boy
with a doleful expression such as is cultivated by young
cantors, was announced as "Sammy Kreitzer, the boy
who now at the age of nine stands as a living example of
the great musical soul of Israel and would have inspired
Shakespeare had the latter lived now or the former lived
before and perhaps then Shylock would never have been
written."

The boy displayed two substantial ankles and played
neither-fish-nor-meat.

"It's a disgrace," Abraham Eiler growled, and wiped
his face.

Max Eiler, the incomparable, refrained from comment,
afraid as he was to be interpreted or misinterpreted,
which amounted to the same. Long ago, listening for the
first time to the masterful playing of Yoakim Herst and
perspiring atrociously, due not so much to gnawing envy
as to the actual heat in the box, he wiped his thinning
head and complained of heat. A famous pianist who sat

next to him affably suggested that the heat was not so oppressive to pianists. The anecdote, embellished and amplified, became a standard story whenever there was talk about Eiler.

Now he simply rubbed his hands, then took off his thick glasses and wiped them. Without spectacles his face was like a ball of putty with a few shrivelled raisins stuck in for effect. Like a Chinese maggot he cocked his head and listened with intense interest to Parrel's Chaconne. The hall seemed to take in the organ-like chords as a dry sponge takes in water.

In the remote corner Vladi dozed, lulled by the mastery of Parrel's bowing. It was amazing, it was incomprehensible that so great a musician should go to waste, that the world should not lie prostrate at his feet, that women should not grow hysterical at the very sight of him. The air quavered with unutterable pathos replete with harmonies. On the crest of the singing waves Ariadne rode into his soul. A strident note arose within his feverish brain and softened into a doleful dirge, a choral strain that transformed the world into a huge cathedral. Tears welled in his eyes. With the haughty flicker of a distant star Ariadne's eyes flashed afar. He saw Bach himself at the organ, austerely engrossed in his overwhelming preludes. Little Bachs, perhaps a hundred of them, were romping around him, tugging at the hem of Ariadne's dress. Like eternity the song rolled out, starting nowhere and striving to no end.

Just then Ariadne entered, followed by Count Rostovtsev and Dr. Kreisel. Eiler quickly fastened his thick glasses on his round nose and nudged his father, who had once upon a distant time been a connoisseur of female charm. Parrel too noticed her arrival and his violin burst out into a veritable pæan and a subtlety of interpretation that made Eiler squirm in his seat, much to the delight of his foes.

Vladi shrank in his dark corner. His head seemed light as a gauze mask. There was the customary clatter of chairs on the stage and the exhilarating cacophony of the tuning of instruments. Ariadne sat down in the first row, flanked by a faun and a satyr. The first violins of the Beethoven Chamber Music Society of New York, mostly hungry looking Germans and Russians, strangely perturbed by her sudden appearance, vied with one another in executing most difficult passages. As if there were any need of further proof of what Anatole France had said about the world revolving around its peculiar axis.

The chaos suddenly gave way to a profound and reverential silence. Kazarinoff's stooped figure wormed its way through the serried rows of eager musicians. He looked tired and exhausted and the baggy swellings under his eyes were ashen-grey. He fidgeted long on the piano stool. His simian arms drooped helplessly between his knees, and he gathered his shoulders and shrank as if he were cold, as if he were freezing under the icy breath of his genius. For a while he sat, morbidly silent. Then his long fingers ran gently over the keyboard, as if to warm themselves. He turned his yellowish face to the conductor and winked.

The dashingly dressed conductor raised his hand, and the orchestra embarked on the majestic Tutti beginning with the unforgettable choral A-C-B-A-G-A-E. A murmur of curiosity ran through the hall: Kazarinoff was playing one of his new compositions.

The conductor, a smug looking German, beside himself with delight, waved his baton, and hushed the strings as soon as Kazarinoff started with the strange lifelessness that was so characteristic of him outside of the concert nights. It was known that he was extremely dull at rehearsals: he was old and afraid to spend the precious fire within him, that divine fire which is allotted but in certain doses, if at all, to humans. This time he was particularly lustreless, and Vladi was bathed in cold perspiration as he watched Ariadne's impassible face. It was evident that she was not interested in the music.

Suddenly, as he wove the net of variations around the languid melody that was the core of the entire Prélude Symphonique, Kazarinoff rose, livid and expressionless, and waved the orchestra into silence.

"Too fast and too strong," he said dully. "And there

must be a tempestuous crescendo in this passage."

"But, my dear Mr. Kazarinoff," the conductor ex-claimed somewhat piqued. *"Es steht doch nicht hier. . . ."*

Kazarinoff lowered his head, as if warding off the scorching sun.

"It is not in the manuscript?" he asked in German with his usual Tartar accent. "No, it isn't . . . Let me see. . . ."

He took the baton and raised his bony hand. As if electrified, the musicians gaped at him, pale and determined not to miss a single detail of this pathetic moment, later to be transmitted to their children and grandchildren. Suddenly he noticed the empty piano stool.

"Is Mr. Corngold here?" he asked amidst a deathly silence.

Vladi gave a start. Ghastly pale, he rose and dragged his lead-shot feet to the stage. His eyes suddenly met Ariadne's. She recognized him and smiled her winsome smile. With an incoherent mumbling he answered her greeting.

Clumsily he climbed on the stage and sat near the piano. His eyes rested beseechingly on Kazarinoff's. As if intoxicated, he threw himself into his musical reverie, forgetting himself, unmindful of the music itself, dangerously near botching everything under the hypnotic spell of her eyes. The luminous aura round her shapely head was his only guide.

When he finished, the hall shook with applause. Kazarinoff coolly nodded to him, and took the place at the piano.

Vladi went off the stage, atrociously conscious of his clumsy dangling arms.

"So you are snubbing us now?" Ariadne said, as he attempted to slip by.

"That's the young genius I introduced to you at one of my soirées," Dr. Kreisel said, patronizingly slapping Vladi on the shoulder and gazing at him with an avid curiosity mingled with wild joy at the thought of the cleverly gotten quartette-manuscript.

In the street, Ariadne slipped her hand under Vladi's arm. The Count trailed behind with Dr. Kreisel. Bewildered, Vladi spoke of his associations with Kazarinoff and the memorable evening he had spent in the pianist's studio. There was a faint curiosity in her eyes, and he suddenly and with pathos spoke of the supremacy of art which made even requited love fade into insignificance. Love was merely a noble stimulus to creative art. The very walls in Kazarinoff's studio had throbbed with joy, as if he had actually caught the underlying melody of life.

Ariadne laughed. "You'll speak differently when you fall in love," she said.

He looked at her with a look of agony. The March sun played on her pallid face. Her lashes threw long shadows, and her steel grey eyes seemed deep and dangerous like mountain lakes. He could never speak to her of his all-consuming passion. To him, his art was merely a stepping-stone to possession of her body and soul. His discourses on the Symphony of Life, his Poem, his Quartette, his Prélude Symphonique seemed vapid, sterile, unnecessary, now that they had achieved their purpose and she walked beside him, reaffirming their intimacy with a gentle pressure.

Her exquisitely carmined lips quivered with faint promise as she remarked casually that Count Rostovtsev would be away in Washington on business.

THE memory of that evening was more gripping than the evening itself.

Like Maya she lay on the couch clad in diaphanous silks that in vain strove to match the alabaster hue of her skin. She did not feel well, she said; she had just emerged from her bath and was still chilly in her flimsy attire; and she wanted him to sit at the piano, so that she could see him the better. A strange foreboding had crept into her heart; and she wanted to gorge herself with his music, for it had a peculiar unearthly quality that brought serenity to her soul.

At her bidding he put out all the lights except the one at the piano, and then improvised in the vein of the Moonlight Sonata. She silently dipped her ethereal handkerchief in the corners of her lovely eyes and even dug her face for a moment in the undulating heaps of grotesque cushions. But she summed up her moods with an amazing reference to his appearance:

"What a pity that your hair is thinning," she exclaimed half-jocularly. "How wonderfully a shock of hair would go with your impetuosity! Sit near me now." And she curled up like an eel and made room for him on the couch.

She wanted him to tell her how he wrote, and whether he really thought of her when he composed his Prélude Symphonique—the one Kazarinoff played with such stirring fervor that the critics almost forgot to comment on the piece itself. He gave vent to his madness and kissed her hands with a sudden boldness.

"You must not," she drawled, putting her head on his knee and gazing up at him as one gazes into the passing clouds on a sultry afternoon.

"Do you really love me?"

"I shall never love anyone but you!" he exclaimed the immortal formula. She loved him, she was near him, and if he could remain there forever and feel the warmth of her body and the encouraging gleam in her eyes, he would demand no more. He spoke to her of the opera he would soon begin, an opera called Ariadne, the symbol of perfect womanhood, the musical incarnation of the union of the body and soul that transforms the world into a magic garden.

She listened, seemingly enthralled, making an attempt to stroke his hair—for a moment she thought she was with Count Rostovtsev—but found not enough support for her nimble fingers and rested them on his cheek with a subdued laugh. He would dedicate the opera, and all he had written before, to her. He dreamed of being her slave and standing in the gallery behind her on a sultry day, fanning her with the huge palm-leaf fan, and silently praying at the sight of her Phryne-like body.

He bent over her and sought her lips—she was so disturbingly near him, and under the yawning slit of the kimono he traced the unmistakable perfection of her body—and suddenly she flung her arms around him and drove her lips into his, seeking to pry them open and thrust out her little tongue to touch his. Her thin silk kimono and the shawl slid away and her nude body throbbed in his arms. He lifted her, gladiator-like, and whispered to her, half-crazed with love. Then he put her back in the groove on the couch still pulsating with her warmth, and sat near her.

"No, no," she cried desperately and slipped out of his embrace, leaving him stupefied and panting.

She stood near the piano lamp, still nude, the kimono wide open, gingerly arranging her hair. He stared at her in agony. Like a siren, near and unattainable, she flashed at him her pearly teeth and round breasts on which the lamp now cast its steady and life-infusing light. He was as near possessing her as he ever was in his dreams, and the pain of it stung his heart. What if he did possess her? He saw her now as he had seen her in his feverish evocations, her breasts, her thighs, her lovely toes playfully drumming on the Chinese rug, her arms lifted, a girlish dawn peeping under her arms through the yawning slits of her kimono. What if she had been his? A feeling of deep frustration swept over him, a feeling that comes into the heart of every man in the wake of possession—and he lowered his head and glumly stared at his knees. In face of this bewildering behaviour, how lucid, how reassuring were his relations with Yashu, and how majestic was the atmosphere of friendship! No wonder men always sought men and later compromised on women.

She sat near him, pleading for brotherly love. He hated her with the hatred of intense passion. He knew little about women, and whatever he knew was romantic, uncertain, and contradictory. The contact with her was like his contacts with the outside world—unenlightening and hasty like his casual affair with Neyla. Beneath the classic perfection of her body he saw wells of primal depth, a depth that he had loved to populate with astounding legends. He loved the dream of her and above all the sudden warmth with which his pen glided on the paper and captured the very essence of her musical self as soon as he evoked her.

"I can't be faithless to the Count," she purred kittenishly, straining his head to hers, and pursing her lips like a dissatisfied and pouting little girl. "He is so noble, even if he is a descendant of generations of cabaret-rioters and mirror-crackers. There is a peculiar depth to his love making, almost elevated to the heights of an art. He has an innate tactfulness and a noble understanding of woman's caprices. Women appreciate that. He leaves me alone when I am in a mood to be alone. He knows I don't love you—and the fact is I don't. But I want you to think of me with all the intensity of your genius, and double my existence in yours."

In her voice he caught the eternal yearning for immortality, the yearning that envenoms human lives and brings them not a step nearer to it. His own restiveness he saw reflected in hers. But she had simply come to the point when the extravagances of passion had become meaningless and even love ominously tepid. Without these life was now singularly purposeless.

She turned to him, and again the silk folds flapped sideways and her nude body pressed to his. He rose and sat at the piano. With a gnawing sadness he realized the kinship of their souls, for that elemental yearning was also his; he too had dreamt of his life kept up eternally in others, a long row of relit torches flaring in the coolness of the night. The whole world was smothered in the pangs of a gnawing hunger that not even possession could appease, for the very word possession stirred up the image of saturation and finality. He had his art to crystallize all the passing moments taut with tragedy; she had to look up to him and barter her loveliness.

As his fingers ran over the keys, these thoughts blended with his musical evocations. Perhaps, as a man he did not exist as far as she was concerned, and his hair was actually thinning. He could not appease her hunger and it was not destined that through him she should come to the bitter aftertaste of disillusionment. But she knew of his love, and she permitted him to love her, and she sought the warmth of his creative power. She had shown him her body and all its alluring mysteries, inconceivable even in dreams.

He played until midnight to Ariadne, who smiled dreamily, her eyes resting on the scores of autographed portraits of celebrities hung on the walls. He was as easy to handle as the rest of them, even though not half as interesting.

Several days later she left with the Count for Moscow.

THE triumph of his Prélude Symphonique and the disappearance of Ariadne were almost simultaneous. Indifferent to the first, he sank in a strange stupor under the weight of the second. He became rather careless about his appearance. He remained without food for a day, until Neyla, alarmed, brought him to his senses. It also became known that he actually threw old Lebenson out of his room when the latter offered him a contract to write the music for a musical comedy entitled A Young American In Paris, "snappy, sexy, jazzy, you know." He wanted to be alone, and it was fortunate that Yashu was on a vaudeville tour, immensely successful, and Feofani was drunk most of the time.

He felt feverish. Crimson faces drew their bluish eyes closer to his and whispered disquieting tales of foreign lands. Ariadne! Ariadne! he moaned, desperately conscious of the huge walls surrounding the deserted city. Way down there were silvery clouds saluting their own shadows cast over green sunlit hills. Before his burning eyes the big parade of shadows passed. Out of the majestic herd one now emerged and whirled and pranced and suddenly tapered into a graceful ethereal column, shapeless yet, but throbbing with potential life hesitant about its next incarnation.

The pillar disappeared. Red light flooded the open spaces and now he swam in tropical doomed waters, keeping shy of a herd of crocodiles snapping their hungry muzzles, ready to tear into the wavering limbs of unwary divers. In palsied frenzy he dropped his limp arms, and fell into the green abyss to a battery of grinning snouts of expectant hippopotami. Toes first, then the whole leg, so snugly entering the contented jejune mugs . . .

Trembling, he woke up, as if cast down the cliff, his heart beating faintly with a cloying sweetness. But he closed his eyes again, and implored sleep to overtake his body, for she was with him, her locks dangling on his chest, her silvery heels tickling in mortal anguish his thighs, and her moonshaped breasts kissing his head. Down they sank past the tremulous reeds, frightening tadpoles. Roaring, he bit his way through the angry water-snakes, and dived mile after mile, Ariadne astraddle of him, the siren, the long-sought-for daughter of Mother-o'pearl. The tadpoles sang meekly in unison, afraid to harmonize and get off pitch:

Will o' the wisp,
Swish by the rushes,
Where the billows lisp,
Where the coral blushes.

And again he was encircled by shoals of cuttles. An abhorrent octopus stretched his tentacles, and sucked the water an inch near him, and then relentlessly dug after his marrow. In one second he passionately engirdled

Ariadne, and dragged her to the argilous cave where he now and then feasted on broken divine girlish limbs.

"Ariadne! Beloved!" he shouted. "Press your lithe body to mine and slip out with me on your eely abdomen through the porthole of the drenched carcass of the brutal leech, and swim, up, up into the azure heights of the calmed surface overshadowed by lianas, where tiny monkeys twit and whir and hum and seesaw on twigs."

At last they were up again. The bluish dim lagoon was hot with drowsy sunset. Her body exhaled flames. "Lie down and float," he said, "I under you, half-crazed with lust, another Atlas sustaining Cosmos, another Jove under his Europa. Let loose your lovely locks, and let them spread like a willowy crown on the zinc surface. Maybe a goldfish will kiss your silky net and I shall die with jealousy."

She rested her oval face on his, and the goldfish sang:

My name is Aruana,
My tail's aglitter.
In blessed Nirvana
Our days we fritter.
Midsummer cobweb,
Gossamer dreams,
World's illusion
Is just what it seems.

Now his pounding veins, his leaden lids and bloodshot eyes and mouth were bursting with liquefied sand. "Let loose, in name of Eros," he cried. "Merge in the Lethal stream, for I'll succumb to torrid witchery created by my own passion . . . And not even the gurgling baby-waves will cool the reeking wounds. Pass on, like the vague flirtation of a curtain in a baby-carriage. Pass on, you daughter of Pan, child of Chimera, ecstatic vision made of burning fire."

Their chariot was slowly passing over the clouds, and her seared, bower-like abdomen no one would now scan with avid eyes. Soon she would die in an orphanage, wizened, his Europa, his own rose-bedecked child, atop the woolly ox, swinging her still lovely amber feet that flanked the benevolent beast. The ox whispered, as he whispered to the child Christ:

Now the moon plays
O'er your beloved locks . . .
Dispassionate rays,
Dull like an ox.
The do-re-mi of water,
The oozing ripples . . .
Press again, beloved,
Your moon-shaped nipples.

The dream was over. A cold wind rose, as if doors had

been quickly opened or the hills sent down the killing gust. It was a beautiful unforgettable dream unfolded to the accompaniment of such perfect harmony that it could never be recaptured in ordinary musical terms. He knew that other dreams were to come. But that delirious scene where he saw himself master of Ariadne, where his life was concurrent with hers to the very last until he invited her to the eternal party given in their honor by the perennial stars atop the firmament,—that dream had assumed all the disturbing elusiveness of reality.

Each and every moment that he was without her now erected a thousand walls between them. Like Hamlet, he spoke to the void. In vain he sought to forget her; it would be futile to cherish a dream. But at night his heart stood still as he peered in the dark behind the vaguely stirring curtains. Yet out of the tormenting ache of his heart he could not conjure up a semblance of Ariadne.

He could no longer stand such overwhelming solitude. Seas and oceans now separated her from him. Yet all the while there was an almost abnormally dogged conviction within him that some day he would meet her; and that all the days leading up to that one sublime moment were of no significance in themselves except that they bridged the gap between the moment he had first seen her and the remote yet certain day when he would meet her again.

To Neyla he feigned normalcy. But as soon as the Revolution broke out, he left for Russia with his violin and a small bundle. Soon he would roam from village to village where birch trees wept over incredibly blue lakes and a lonely lustreless star, reflected a thousandfold, glided in the translucent and fragrant air to the opposite pole of the unfathomed universe. Like a particle of that universe, in its every manifestation, Ariadne beckoned him from afar, ever present, like a liquescent delicacy digested by the cosmos and kept circulating in its mighty blood-stream, and in accordance with its tension changing the tempo, pulse and blood-pressure of future lives . . .

Back in Moscow he found nothing but desolation. His father and mother had been slain in a street riot in Moscow during the first bloody outbursts of the Revolution. Yet there was no resentment in his soul. His great mission had overshadowed everything else.

In the rising chaos, he perceived nothing but shadows. Dusk enshrouded the earth. Cloudy vapors hung over it like misty spirits conjured by witchcraft. The whole world was palsied. Strange maladies and freaks made their appearance. Men fell asleep and slept for months. In one town a woman gave birth to a child of canine face and claws. The number of children born with cleft noses grew to alarming proportions. Over the roads beggars prowled chanting lays and prophecies based on the revelations of the Apocalypse. The foul breath of the Antichrist swept over the soil. The grass withered and the trees stood in gaunt wickedness. Strange things were happening. There were rumors of a huge man in the South who could stop the circulation of his blood at will. At a meeting of his followers he had cut off one of his ears without a trace of blood. The air was surcharged with stories of miracles compared with which those of medieval saints appeared tricks of a second-rate magician at a county-fair. Overnight, people grew rich. Every man was a potential Napoleon. Children dug in the earth for an apple-core, and stumbled on fabulous treasures. Next day these artless discoverers were massacred and their riches confiscated by many greedy hands. Gold, silver, and precious stones were found in the streets; priceless paintings were found pasted inside soldiers' trunks. A Rembrandt, stolen from the Hermitage was discovered in a tavern toilet and bought for ten roubles, then smuggled abroad and sold for three million francs. Entire streets were paved with malachite, jade, and marble. The spirit of adventure wafted over the Ural mountains and like a playful breeze pervaded the vast prairies of Russia. All bonds were severed. Young men and women armed themselves, joined brigands, and changed their lives into a glamorous fairy tale.

Nothing could stem the elemental human deluge, not even the ten thousand executions a day, the quartering, the flaying alive, and the slow-fire torture. On the outskirts of towns thousands of bodies were hastily dumped into a huge grave, and the tumulus, like the barren dug of a starved cur, slowly sagged under the corroding breath of nocturnal cold. Days of the Inquisition, the quiet, smug and arrogant murderousness of Medieval clerics had returned. All eyes were ablaze with depravity.

Admiral Kolchak was in Kazan. The fall of Moscow was said to be imminent. A desperate call to arms was issued by the Reds who had completely lost their heads. The streets, the houses, the cellars were overrun with deserters. Every week a new government was set up here and there, and on every street corner people were executed for failing to comply with the orders of some petty commandant.

Twice he was on the verge of such a fate. Once a box of matches saved him. Together with two other fugitives caught in the street by two drunken Calmucks intent on tasting human blood, he was placed against a wall. One man was shot. The other fell on his knees and bellowed hysterically. A huge crowd gathered on the opposite sidewalk and watched the performance. The Calmuck loaded the revolver and fired a bullet through the man's ear. Vladi stood, pale, rigid, unconscious. The drunken Calmuck stopped and leisurely rolled a cigarette. As he turned to the other executioner for a match, bickering in his screechy Mongolian voice, Vladi quickly darted around the corner and, escaping three or four shots, disappeared in the market place.

At another time he was flung into a rathole and fought famished brazen rats until dawn. Like a hunted beast he eluded the forces of man and nature. From Ariadne and music he drew his strength, the will to live, and resistance. He could not die. It seemed unthinkable that he should perish before reaching his goal. A sort of fatalistic confidence buoyed up his spirits. With a bullet in his heart he would still live and breathe and reach out to the sun. He was immortal in his madness.

Once he was arrested by the advance guard of a White detachment and, together with two dozen nondescripts was sentenced to be executed. Along the rearing walls of a cloister, complete like a crushing jail of Van Gogh, they were huddled; just converging walls, and thirty men. The afternoon was dreary. It had rained and the ground was muddy. They passed before him, one man with a beard, a Jew, the other in leggings, the third with a nude torso. Still another, a very old man, swathed in rags, and then a mulatto, like a nightmare.

"Come in!" someone shouted. The din in his ears was like approaching thunder. The tall officer in a huge Cossack shako smiled at them.

"Nice picnic," he said. "Come in, boys."

One of them, the bearded fellow was shot down. "Ai-ai!" he shrieked and crumbled up in a heap.

The soil was soggy like a cemetery on a steamy June day after rain.

His knees trembled. A minute passed. And yet it might be quite pleasant, at the end of this weary long journey, to be put out of the way, to be placed in noiseless layers of atmospheric pressure, to float.

The very old man wrapped in warm rags turned out to be an old woman, hiccoughing and fussing senilely.

"Old Woman!" she shouted. "Woman! Woman! . . . Grand-d-d-children!" she snarled hysterically. One, two, three. The mechanism of her life ceased to function. Her face vanished in the heap of rags, the gear had broken and the cogs no longer fitted snugly in the familiar grooves.

No, he was not afraid. He would be out in a minute, just like a frolicsome urchin, playing his part in an entrancing hide-and-seek. But, meanwhile, where would all the sounds of his soul linger? All the skill, all the fine-gauged scales, all the intricate precision of divinely inspired fingers! He might live in Ariadne, even as she would continue to live in him were she to disappear forever.

The mulatto in front of him screamed: "I am happy to die for the Communists! . . . Long live the brotherhood of man! . . . I despise . . ."

His white heart ceased beating, his black body lay lifeless in the snow. He was the thirty-third.

Vladi was alone. He closed his eyes. He felt slain. He lay prostrate on top of the heap, killed anew a thousand times over. All the sounds that ever enshrouded his heart were suddenly released. Presently, he opened his eyes. He was still erect. The hangman stared at him; his lips were blue, his eyes yellow, his hair grey, and his face olive-green from the breath of Death. The man slowly raised the huge revolver.

"Are you Vladi Corngold?" the man spoke eagerly.

"Yes," he answered and his trembling voice clung to the dreary cloister yard, blue with shadows, purpled with trickling blood; then, strangely modulated, the voice was wafted back to him.

"Heavens!" the officer whispered. "You—here?"

"Yes," he repeated, trembling. "Yes. Yes. Yes!"

"Were you ever in the St. Petersburg Conservatory?" the officer asked, dropping the revolver.

"Yes," he repeated again. His teeth chattered. He could utter no sound other than *da-da-da-da*.

"You, the pupil of Leopold Auer?"

"*Da-da-da-da* – Like a machine gun his teeth clicked."

"Oh, what are you doing here?" the hangman whispered. "Go home . . . go home. . . ."

He handed him a gun and a pass. Vladi turned and went to the gate of the monastery.

"Show me your fingers," the officer asked, and stared

vacantly at them for a while, and touched them with a morbid curiosity.

"How wonderfully you used to play! As long as I live, so help me God, I shan't forget your music. . . . Such fingers. . . . Go!"

"Who are you?" he asked. He was alive, breathing fever.

"I am the janitor's son," the other answered. "Go home."

"Go home! Go home! Go home!" he shouted, the blood pounding at his temples, and his throat so dry that his tongue was numb.

And he reeled out into the bleeding spaces.

The soil was crimson, the rain as salty as a teardrop. And the wind prodded him on like the tragic chords of his own Poem. He sang with the wind, seized by its twirling impact.

It was just this stupendous background that he had dreamt of for his quest of Ariadne.

THREE times he felt her presence in the catastrophic turmoil.

He had followed her from city to city on the flimsiest of clues, always late, always fatally detained by explosions, crumbled bridges, derailed trains, and meetings of railroad officials. Like a caterpillar the train crept uphill, stopping at an obscure station in the steppe and halting for five or ten hours. Huddled in the corner of a jammed car, he gazed patiently through the open window. Twilight was aquiver in the quiescent balmy air. The dark station-house would soon bestir itself, belching forth weird shadows and blood-curdling images. An old peasant with a long shreddy beard stared resignedly at a huge cloud that like a buxom woman with a glowing broom swept the other clouds aside and cleared a place for herself. Tucked away into every celestial corner, there were tufts of cottony vapors, blanched with indignation, yet so immaculate that the straggling white lambs in other corners turned green with envy. Presently the whole sky turned green, incredibly green, except where the buxom woman, leaning on her orange broom, held sway. Then came dusk. The peasant, like an old stinted bush, stood in the dark. The engine puffed weakly, and a star, and another, and then the whole army of them twinkled in the blessed southern night. Toward dawn the train would slowly resume its caterpillar motion.

His Poem was his last resort. Perhaps his name would

attract her attention and she would come and recall that unforgettable evening when she was almost his.

The nascent horrors of the Civil War were scarcely conducive to musical activities. Yet, perhaps just because everything else was crumbling and assumed the tragic transiency of a human life, there was a rather large audience that had braved the bullets and occasional street skirmishes. The orchestra, weary and half-starved, played with a sudden abandon of which only Russians are capable. Nathan Miller, the *Wunderkind*, played the Poem with unique fervor. Visibly stirred, a young woman who sat next to Vladi, asked him if he knew anything about Vladi Corngold. He shook his head distractedly. The oval face in the front row was not Ariadne's!

Another time, at a chance street meeting he heard the name of Count Rostovtsev rabidly flung into the crowd by an infuriated orator, who denounced aristocratic leeches and their hangers-on. Later, he read in the papers that a Count Rostovtsev perished at the headquarters of General Dukhonin when the general himself was torn to pieces. Beyond doubt, it was the same Rostovtsev who was a military attaché in Washington and later Kerenski's right hand and military adviser. At last she was free.

A hasty trip to the scene of tragedy definitely confirmed the rumors of the Count's death. Also, that Ariadne was on her way to Arkhangel, which the Allied

Expeditionary Forces now vaguely hoped to make the base of a new colossal anti-Red offensive. He heard there were also Americans among them.

For the third and last time he came face to face—not with her, but with the memory of her.

An uncertain clue led him to the house of Fabian Lossin, the futurist and stormy petrel of new music, of whom he had heard when still a child, now an outburst of admiration, now a smirk of contempt.

He found the man in his murky room, leaning against the wall cribbed with an unexpected growth of ivy and a profusion of branches stuck in the corner. A tamed squirrel now hopped along now rolled away like a skein of yarn. The stooped man with the hydroptic face and walrus mustache gazed at him expectantly.

"I am . . . I am a friend . . . of yours . . . and a friend of . . . Rostovtsev . . . Count Rostovtsev . . ." he muttered.

"The one killed at the headquarters?" Lossin asked, calmly rubbing his palms and puffing childishly.

"Yes. It was a horrid sight, and it is painful for me to recall it," he lied, and dropped on the tabouret, which careened and sent him reeling on his back.

"Pardon us," Lossin said as calmly as before, "we are using up our wood gradually. But it does not matter. Sit down at the piano, we haven't used that up yet. What is the nature of your visit?"

"Ariadne!" he exclaimed. "I came to find Ariadne."

"I really don't know," Lossin drawled, catching the squirrel and setting it between his knees. "I've seen her but once in my life. . . ."

A very ugly woman in a drab skirt and spotted blouse quickly entered the room.

"We don't know where she is," she said quickly and bitingly. "How are we supposed to know where she lives and who you are?"

"I see you don't trust me," he muttered sadly. "If I could only convince you that I played with Kazarinoff and that he himself played my Prélude Symphonique in New York!"

"So you are a musician?" the woman inquired.

"Yes. And now it seems to me that my entire life depends on whether I'll find Ariadne or not."

"It only seems so," Lossin said casually, stroking the cunning little animal.

"Why?" the woman suddenly exclaimed. "I can understand such great and all-consuming passion."

"The passion will also pass," Lossin said benevolently. Vladi looked round him with sudden calmness, as if he had felt the breath of Ariadne in that room. He spoke of Miska Szabai, and Auer, and Parrel, and the rehearsals, then switched to the Poem and Feofani. They listened silently and indifferently to the message from another world until he mentioned the last name. They had known

Feofani in his heyday when he was the undisputed lord of the Conservatory and gladdened everybody's heart with obscure Armenian jokes and merry stories.

A deep silence ensued, as if they were mourning the sudden disappearance of the behemoth and bemoaned his absence. Vladi spoke sadly of the downfall of Feofani, and the two listened with a sorrowful satisfaction, for even they resented his amazing climb to glory.

"I remember having seen you in Rostov, when they played your sonata for cello and small orchestra. They panned it mercilessly, didn't they?"

"Thank goodness," Lossin sighed. "That was the happiest day of my life: at last I was completely misunderstood."

"Don't mind what he says," the woman said. "Ariadne is on her way to Arkhangel. You don't intend to follow her, do you?"

"Yes, indeed," he exclaimed. "I shall leave to-day. I have followed her like a dog that has lost its master. But always late—an hour, a day, a week—does it matter? But fatally late. Tell me of her, you who have seen her so often."

"You'll never reach Arkhangel," she retorted. "You'll be executed in the first burg. The roads teem with spies. And you don't seem very practical."

"Oh yes, I am," he cried out. "I am very, very cunning.

I derive all my cunningness from her. She is perfection itself. Everybody loves her."

And he quickly lifted the lid and burst into a triumphant scherzo from his unwritten symphony.

"It's foolish to love so fiercely," Lossin interrupted his effusions. "Such love encroaches on freedom. And freedom is the one sublime goal of mankind, for it leads to extinction. Does not freedom lead to revelation? And whatever is revealed dies from exposure and the deadening glance of evil eyes."

"Beautiful love and beautiful music," the woman said softly, and her thick underlip dropped. "You mustn't mind everything my husband says. He has his points of insanity."

"Everyone has," Vladi assented, laughing happily. The murky room was now aglow with an even soft light that seemed to emanate from the autographed portraits of Glazounoff, Auer, Stravinski, Prokofieff and scores of others. In this very room Ariadne had sat and touched the piano keys and spoken. As if in a trance, he spoke to them of his dream and the exotic madness that had overtaken him and driven him to the pier. He had swum in an unbelievable blue lagoon hot with drowsy sunset and crocodiles were then fighting for his bones. Now and then the dream recurred with an ever-increasing clarity, silencing the insipid distant tunes that threatened to disrupt the magic harmony of his vision. The very trees sang in unison, then *divisi*, and he had tried in vain to recapture that balmy melody ever since. Perhaps another dream, more colorful than this one, might turn into music and linger forever in his soul.

"For whom must you recapture it?" Lossin asked. "No one will ever hear the sounds you hear or see the dreams you see. The world sings to you, and to you alone, for you can attune your heart to the harmony that emanates from a distant star. Others will never understand. Write for yourself, if you wish, like the Provençal troubadours in their *trobar clus*, or the Kavya poets in India. This is true freedom and true extinction."

"I am different" Vladi softly said. "Yet we speak the same language, even if to different ends. To me life is nothing but a dream, and art is the memory of that dream. And isn't the memory of a thing sweeter than that thing itself? You seek extinction, and I seek immortality, which is, after all, the same. And the true immortality of the thing is in the memory of it."

"Beautiful words," the woman whispered, looking greedily at him. "Please, do not mind my husband. He is very distraught ever since our son died."

"Most amazing lie I ever heard," Lossin calmly proceeded. "Our son was a maniac and drug-addict. I am really happy he died."

"He isn't," the woman stammered and tears rolled

down her wrinkled cheeks. "Death is almost as terrifying as life."

"I am not afraid of death," Vladi said firmly, and rose. "A thousand times each minute we confront death in the falling of a leaf, in the rustle of silk, in the vanished smile, in the dried-up tear, in the disrupted cloud. Do you think that a vanished life is more disturbing than a vanished smile or the sudden whiff of sweet odor brought by the evening breeze? For should I die in my quest of Ariadne, the wind will carry on my tale. Or perhaps, you."

"Never," Lossin whispered almost imperceptibly. His face was now very pale and his mustache covered his chin as if veiling its telltale quiver.

"Who shall tell? The world is so miraculously interwoven,—and whether we want it or not, our image is reflected somewhere and lingers, and lingers, until the mirror is broken."

"Oh, stay here with us," the woman suddenly cried out. "Think of the horrid North!"

"I must go," he said resolutely. "I cannot live without her. She is life."

"Don't go," she clutched at him desperately. "There are villages in the remote North that are infested with midgets and lepers and cannibals. The world is wicked, and famine steels hearts and minds. They know of no law human or divine."

"I shall manage somehow," he said. "I'll find her."

"She may be on her way to America."

"I'll join her there."

He kissed the woman's hand and shook hands with her husband. The squirrel ran up to his knee and stared into his face imploringly.

"May God help you," Lossin said with difficulty. "I shall be thinking of what you said. I am very tired now, but to-morrow I shall start on my cycle of songs: Voices that Are Heard in the Desert."

The door closed gently behind him.

He wended his way Northward, to the White Sea and the marshy tundra. Summer was unusually hot that year, and many prisoners died in the catacombs before dates had been set for their execution. Yet even on placid days he felt a cold wind stinging the nape of his neck. Bony fingers pointed at him. Red-bearded, malevolent faces stared at him, hiccoughing their foul breath. He was buffeted about in military trains, and, like a pilgrim, he trudged over deserted roads. Had he been caught, he would have been executed. But he looked old, very old. In a false passport his age appeared as forty-five; and his long beard made him look that old. When his violin, his sole treasure, a gift from his lamented parents, was stolen from him, he really grew old overnight.

He became taciturn. A gripping sadness overwhelmed

him. In his nervousness, he felt a maddening desire to leap from the train, cart, or char-à-bancs, and dash his head against the cold earth. Everywhere he saw human figures with pig-like faces rushing about, pell-mell. There are moments in life when one suddenly realizes his insignificance and the eternal unimportance of the whole world as well. Whether amidst the raging tempest or when the sun sets in placid waters and spreads its glowing smile over the innocent azure, one suddenly shakes with despair. Whatever one's insight, whatever one's experiences and contacts, one trembles with cold fear, as if he were about to be executed. A strange and distant voice, like the lament of an oboe, or a casual wail of a shepherd horn in the mountains pierces the heart with the sting of a venomous snake and one falls to the ground and buries his face in his hands and cringes before the horrid power that blindly tosses him about.

He felt the breath of that power: it was the breath of this Infinite, the silent mystery of a cloudy shadow realigning itself on the inviting hillock on a sultry day. Like the messenger of the Infinite she was. He saw her again and again, desperately hitching her to some semblance of reality that might bring her down on earth and infuse a cooling rigidness into her forms. She was self-sufficient in her beautiful purposelessness, and her sudden disappearance might be as inexplicably puzzling as her appearance.

Before long, he was beyond the reach of disintegrating law and order. Moscow was hundreds of miles behind him. And there were no cities ahead. Now and then, unobtrusively, he passed through sleepy villages, begging alms to the tune of ditties. But soon even such drab adventures failed to relieve the monotony of his pilgrimage. As he walked over the snow-clad plains in the North, where the roads are impassable even in Summer, groping his way to Arkhangel, he saw himself as the flickering projection to which Debussey's *Reverie* had been composed. In the mournful sough of the Northern wind he discerned the eight-note cluster accompaniment into which overlapping notes wove a plaintive rustic wail, as if the tired soul of a crushed girl were tarrying a moment for help. Whenever he played that *Reverie*, which he himself had transcribed for the violin, he beheld the delicate face of Ariadne who had vanished so strangely, so tracelessly. He wondered why people did not create a greater stir when making their exit! A sound, to linger in his ears, to tint sweet memories! He was really unpretentious, so easy to satisfy! A mere smile from her would make his heart beat more vigorously, and cast such a radiance into his soul that the snow around him would suddenly assume the weird exuberance of tropical beauty . . .

As he roamed through the treacherous marshy plains, shunned by the two or three peasants he encountered, he succumbed to the hypnotizing monotony of the endless North. The very enchantment of the Antarctic landscape revived his strength. At night, chattering from cold, he whispered the eternal refrain: Ariadne . . . Ariadne . . . And as he began to doze, soft voices commingled with the nascent wind.

Before long he had a companion, a droll and lovely cub-bear he had found in the forest hopelessly entangled in brushwood. He shared his bread and salt with the animal. Then they wended their way north, restless specks creeping over the snow.

Long were the nights before the fuming and crackling brushwood. The snow fell in dense flakes. Age-old trees muttered, their tops defiantly bowed under the fury of the gale. The vanishing flames merged with the darkness congealing into mocking outlines.

At dawn he washed his face with snow. The bear did likewise. It was a precious trick, and he had her repeat it several times until the cub was ready to do it at his bidding. Then they turned back to the forest, and again resumed their eternal march northward, to Ariadne.

Far away, the black scraggly protuberances waved their bushy heads to him. The monotony of the Northern landscape wrought its deadening imprint on his mind. An overwhelmed calm filled his soul. Like an eternal wanderer in these swampy regions he was, one who had never before known warmth and supple bodies on Southern shores.

The sudden advent of the negro, monstrously incongruous as it was, did not immediately strike him. In those days there probably had been no more than a dozen negroes in all Russia, mostly vaudeville actors, wrestlers, and cooks. This one was ragged and starved, with a sickly green rigid face. His eyes glistened with morbid hostility. His cool greeting ended with a spasmodic coughing, and all pretense was abandoned as soon as he saw the flask. So great was his thirst that he bit his tongue and squealed like an old cur on whose tail a cruel boot has stepped.

Vladi looked at his brutal nostrils, at his shaking body wrapped in rags of most incoherent coloring, and suddenly before his eyes rose the half-dimmed greyish face of one great mulatto who fell down with his banner in the inquisitorial yard of a Monastery.

"I am going to Arkhangel," he said with a sudden quiver, shuddering under the tragic memories of that afternoon. "You can join me if you wish."

The negro defiantly asked for another drink, eyeing the bear suspiciously. It was evident that a sordid past gnawed at his mind and prodded him on to seek men and speak to them, to deafen the insane mutterings of another being within him. He told amazing tales of power and glory. The stories were essentially the same and there were no discrepancies even in the details. He had been a man of influence and ingenuity. If it had not been for a rather unfortunate concurrence of circumstances, he would still wield power equal to that of the Governor of a State. But he had fallen under the wheel of the Juggernaut of Revolution. At night he crept into a village and pretended to be a ghost and moaned and robbed the peasants, and roared with humiliation . . .

Lashed by the north winds they plunged into the snowy hills. The menacing façade of the forest filled his heart with terror, benumbing his mind with its icy breath. For miles around lay white plains, monotony broken by grotesquely jutting firs or dwarfish bushes. Not a soul.

When they saw a man, they squatted and made believe they were part of the foggy scenery of the North. Minds are distrustful and hostile in that region of eternal struggle. Not infrequently they had to bow before sheer force. It is a matter of common knowledge that the demon of the Northerners is black; and Paradise would be too drab a place for one credited with killing the negro and thus delivering the world from the advent of the Antichrist.

Not all encounters were humiliating. More than once they succeeded in executing Tom's stratagem. Imminent starvation inclined their minds to scheming. After a long squabble, the negro killed the cub-bear and broiled it. Then there came a day when they were left without food and cartridges, and they lay for half a day waiting for some mad bird to hop within reach of the hatchet. Evening came and they still were without food. The negro growled.

All night long, close by the smouldering embers, the negro snorted and writhed and guffawed, filling the forest with such terror that Vladi stared at him with agony. For eight days they had been travelling together, and each night the negro threw his wild exorcisms into the dark. Blood on the stony floor, brains splattered over grim walls and oozing into this great forest, making the woolly beasts of the slumbering North shiver with horror. The dead were stirring in their tombs into which they had been cast while still alive. He was the image of Naaman, the hangman in Wilde's Salome. He had been a hangman. He made no bones about his erratic past. He had come to Russia to have a white woman and assert his equality with the white race. He became a chef in a minor club in Batum, and fared well. But this was not the liberty he had dreamt of. With the first outbreak of the Revolution he joined the Communists. His very grotesqueness, and the fact that he spoke in the name of millions of slaves of detested capitalism, made him a persona grata at all meetings and demonstrations. He became famous. Women, white and beautiful sought him. He held a responsible post with the Cheka—he was one of the chief executioners. The very sight of him was so horrifying that victims fainted in his presence and facilitated the job for the under-executioner.

There were thousands like him who thought the Red Revolution was a picnic. All his life he had dreamt of equality and whiteness; when these had come, he was dazzled. A slave all his life, he could not readjust himself. After the Reds left, he was slashed by an infuriated mob and dragged to the post. The fact that he was an American citizen saved his life. With the brazenness of despondency he demanded to be delivered to the American representative in Constantinople. The Whites offered him the post of executioner instead. He accepted; he had thought the Reds had been driven out forever, and he was as murderously efficient with the White as with the Reds. Soon the Reds came. The shore was guarded, and he hid in the interior.

The negro spoke drowsily, as if dreaming, unmindful of the moaning trees. His bulging eyes were red, and purple shadows played over his haggard face. Vladi rose to stir up the fire and add fuel. His motion was so brisk that the negro jumped to his feet as if ready to ward off a blow.

"What do you want?" he screamed at the top of his lungs, and the whole forest laughed, as if invisible beasts jeered at them, stretching out and licking their greedy tongues. Shrill was his cry and sudden. Vladi looked at the fire with a morbid concentration as if seeing the bronze body of the hangman grilling over the glowing embers. Then he fell back and growled:

"What are you hollering about? Do you want to get into trouble?"

"Oh, what a nightmare! What a terrible nightmare!" the negro muttered. "How it grips my soul!" And he lapsed into a disjointed narrative of the sweet episodes of his life in Baku where there are such lovely Persian girls with fiery henna-tinged hair and nails, and where he married a Georgian princess. She had a noble nose and lips like a statue and her arms were like snakes. She was so miraculously beautiful that his knees trembled when he beheld her. She stood in the corner of the dungeon where he had seen so many come and pass away forever. He took off his mask, and she uttered a dreadful scream. Was he really so ugly that people shuddered at the mere sight of him? Ugly or not, she was in his hands, and she understood it. He walked over to her, took her hands in his, and asked her to kiss him. Her lifeless lips whispered prayers. Then she fainted. He took her down to an underground passage and there kept her for a week. Like a rat she lived there in the cellar, and he brought her food and wine and slept with her. Every night she belonged to him, she, the daughter of a Caucasian prince.

"Eulalia was her name, and a sweet name it was," he mumbled and groaned under the weight of the tragic fate of his love affairs. A faint epileptic froth simmered at the corners of his mouth. To the crackling flames he spoke deliriously, for Vladi no longer listened, weeping bitterly, like a child. He loved art, and he longed for Ariadne, and he had no interest in the rest of the world; why then had he so often been drawn into blood, wickedness, death? An unappeased solitude burned in his heart. On the threshold of the great tundra where stags, stirring their beautiful antlers, desperately search for a piece of lichen and dig for hours with their slender legs, how alone he was, not strong enough to be sustained even by the glamorous vision of that ethereal girl!

Without compass, without guide, companion of an executioner, he sat near the dying fire invoking the spirit of love that seemed to pervade the noble night.

Soon there were three of them, and the hostile snows seemed less treacherous to his heart.

The stranger's name was Atmashov, Atma for short. He was a Cheremiss from the Volga region, but spent most of his time in the North practising quack medicine and veterinary surgery. As he was wending his way toward Arkhangel, he had nothing against joining them, for "one head is good and two are better."

September was drawing to a close and the air was pure and bracing. Sometimes the sun in a quick flash, like an icy disc, coolly breathed upon the scintillating plain. The great snowy North sang in cold quints and fourths with the mystic musical proportions that no one but Grieg had overheard.

Atma led the way; of the three he knew the North best. He felt keenly his unity with Nature. He could predict the future; but mostly attributed his skill to the teachings of his master Ibrahim of Biskra. He had roamed all over the world as a sailor, until nostalgia drove him back to his native plains. The world was his.

He needed little, and had just as much as he needed. In the negro he felt not so much a personal enemy as a man who stood for all he, Atma, denied. Twice he suggested that they drop the black hangman and let him shift for himself, for, so he said, "the lines on his hand clearly indicate quick death." Vladi, stirred to the core, hesitated.

Night came. They halted and built a fire. A storm was not improbable, Atma said. For a while they were silent. The negro complained of a strange pain in his leg, and whimpered like a child. He was afraid of the night. Already at the first inroads of twilight he had grown fidgety. How restless, how cringing he became with the first sad message of dusk! At night his cowardice verged on panic. He sat almost in the very middle of the woodpile, as if he thrived on infernal heat.

"Gosh, I hate them nights," he mumbled.

The Cheremiss stirred the fire and stared at the flames like a mummy. Not a thought could be read on his rigid face.

Vladi moved closer to the fire and tucked himself into the blanket. Soon he fell asleep. He dreamed that he heard a deep, even voice slowly groping its way to the blue crown of the forest: "Glue them together . . . How do you do . . . Oh, what a long beard . . . The sword is sure to catch in your Jewish whiskers . . . One, two, chik . . . No more beard, no more barber shop. But it was all a mistake, of course . . ."

"Why a mistake?" he exclaimed with feverish excitement, waking up with a suddenness that almost shoved his body into the flame. He was still half asleep. All sense of reality gone, he spoke to the delirious negro. He forgot for a while that he was more alone than ever; it was immaterial, in face of the inexhaustible possibilities of the universe. Like an actor in an engrossing melodrama, he subsisted on his pent-up ecstasies. The stage was set. A cooling wave rowelled his flesh, sneaking into the stomach and tickling it into the despair of impending death, the most blissful sensation of suspense. What was death? Just one step further in that mint-flavored coolness. The main thing was to live down all fears and plunge into the very vortex of madly jostling waves. The essential thing was to impersonate as many parts as possible and rehearse the thousand and one reincarnations before the final falling of the curtain.

He stroked his wavy beard and softly spoke to Atma about his dreams. There was no sadness in his heart. What was next? He was atremble with curiosity.

They had scarcely walked half a mile, when Tom cried out with a curse:

"My foot! . . . Oh, how it hurts! Feels like I'd stubbed my toe on a rusty nail!"

They stopped to help him unwind the rags he had wrapped around his patched leggings. There was a nail protruding from his swollen messy toe. Atma pulled it out with a quick jerk, and black blood trickled across the snow like a newborn snake. Then he bandaged the foot with the cleaner parts of his shirt.

They stretched him on a litter of pine branches. As he

lifted him, Atma puckered his thin lips and whispered: "He won't live long. Let's leave him here."

"Whatcha saying there?" Tom shouted. "Come on, let's go."

"Yes, we are going," Vladi hastened to calm him, unable to repress the feeling of pity which the sickly grey face evoked in him. He hated the negro with all the might of his reason, and he loved him in a vague, unaccountable, emotional way. Was he not of the same race with Ariadne? As one loves the brother, the dog, the clothes of the woman one loves,—thus he was attracted to the negro.

He lifted the fore end of the litter, and they moved. The Cheremiss chanted: "Dreadful death, oh, dreadful death . . . A big kettle full of boiling water and man hanging down in thin strips . . ."

"Oh, what a song," Tom groaned. "Give me a drink, I got a helluva thirst."

He was growing delirious. His foot was swollen, and they had to change the bandage every half hour; the gangrenous wound was a nauseating sight. But his will to live was overwhelming. In his ravings he saw himself back in Harlem, in his best clothes, leaning over the counter and swapping yarns with the flower of the neighborhood.

Twilight emerged to meet them. They walked alongside the deep forest. Exhausted by the heavy burden, they trudged on hopelessly until night fell. The negro was dozing. They set down the litter. He opened his eyes.

"Still here?" he asked huskily. "My throat is burning."

"Wait a moment," Vladi said. "We'll cut some wood, clean the ground, and camp here for the night."

"No camp, no camp," the negro roared, and made a move to run. But pain and long slumber had paralyzed him. He fell back, and tears of agony glistened in his eyes.

Morning came. They ate the last bits of bread and drank boiled snow. Then they picked up the litter and again plunged into the boundless prairies.

The wind raged and the trees bent low. With the gust came the monotonous droning of an endless melody: "Here he comes, Orka the Great, Spirit of Evil, Spirit of Earth. He tramples on men, he enters women, he devours children, for He is great. From beneath the earth, like a vapor, he oozes out and treks over the exhausted surface of mother earth, and he enters through my reeking gashes and then I see Him, Atma sees the world to come . . . And then I relate to you the mysteries of Orka."

"Atma! Atma!" Vladi shouted. "What are you singing?"

The silky snowflakes crept into his mouth, became glued to his face and froze to his eyelashes. White like Saint Nicholas, Atma was before him.

"Walk, walk," the voice came through the furious gale. "You mustn't stand still in a storm. On, on."

But he could not extricate himself from the deep snow. The eerie chant still rang in the air, and he felt an irrepressible somnolence gripping him and slowly driving him into the engulfing snow.

Atma dragged him out of the ravine and they turned back to the forest, where the snow was not so dense. There they deposited the litter and found shelter in a quickly improvised small cabin. The fire they managed to build near the entrance cheered them somewhat.

Thus they lay huddled together under the branch pile. Though in the forest the storm was not so terrifying as in the plains, the very trees seemed to be disintegrating. Now and then a big clod of frozen snow fell from the tree-tops to the shaky roof of the cabin, threatening to crush it. White visions thrust forth their hoary arms. Witches made an attempt to put out the fire.

Atma squatted under the branches, and pale reflexes of the fire played round his squinting eyes. His sparse, black little beard, in which every hair could be traced, was tightly clutched in his bony fingers. His body swayed with monotonous cadences to the undulating howls of the sweeping gale. He sang his endless tune.

A dancing wall of iced old women, a devilish carousal of meheras enraged in their sterile widowhood, twirled round them.

"Cover me, cover me," the negro moaned. "It's damn cold, too cold to live. They're stirring in their graves and their white bones rustle like wood. How about a drink? A drink, I said. The drink is red, all red . . ."

He sobbed convulsively, and suddenly his moist eyes fell on Vladi, and he stammered through his clenched teeth:

"Brother, come nearer to me . . ."

"What does he say, the black one?" Atma asked. "How red are his eyes! His foot is dead, and soon the rest of him will be dead. We'll have to cut it before we reach the village."

And they passed through the storm-ridden screen into the pearly mist of the horizon.

A STRANGE village it was, and no human being is likely to believe the story I am about to tell. The men wore long tufted beards, as if they had definitely decided to protect at least parts of their faces from the biting cold of long winters. Their eyes were like steel, and their hearts full of murderous desires. They had a queer sense of humor. They thought nothing of sending a man a hundred miles away to hunt for a non-existent inheritance. Once they actually convinced a credulous old man that he was dead and persuaded him to creep into a crudely made coffin. Over the supposedly dead body they chanted prayers and begged God to have mercy on the sinful soul of the departed. Thereupon the shaking, half-conscious body was carried to the cemetery and slowly lowered into a freshly dug grave, until the priest's helper, a semi-literate student of a religious school, struck the old corpse and proclaimed majestically: "Arise, Lazarus!"

Their jokes were extremely cruel, but they enjoyed them none the less. Once a young peasant who happened to pass through the village, asked one of the men in the street how to get to Gvozdevo. They told him to wait and pretended to hurry off to the chief for information.

Soon they returned, trundling a huge barrel studded with nails within. They shoved the poor peasant into the barrel and rolled the reluctant Diogenes downhill until he turned into a horrid mass of bleeding flesh.

"There is your Gvozdevo," they jested good-naturedly (Gvozd is Russian for nail). But this touch of playful brutality was lost on the victim. He died that very same evening. No one ever inquired about him, and he was soon forgotten.

It was at once apparent that these hale, carefree animals were possessed of a tremendous playfulness that had to be gratified somehow. They had never heard of theatre, for the nearest town was two hundred miles away. They knew nothing about motion pictures, phonograph, radio, or telegraph. And when later told about these, they became as angry as wild boars, believing no doubt, that one had made sport of them.

Yet they were ever bent on venting their elemental exuberances. They always fought: in jest, of course. But now and then the joke would end tragically. The Law could never reach them; they were absolute masters of their village, not unlike despotic Asiatic satraps. There was no constituted authority to be found for miles around.

To be sure, various attempts had been made to subdue these mischievous villagers. Once a Soviet tax-collector entered the village, but no sooner had his mission been revealed, than he was killed. For quite a while they were successful in hiding every trace of the crime, and even sent apparently authentic reports, in the name of the dead official—the village notary being an expert forger. They finally informed the district Soviet that the tax-collector had been drowned while bathing in the river. Naturally, the Soviet discredited the report and sent a commission of three to investigate the situation, exhume the body, and punish the guilty ones. But the body could not be found. When the newcomers insisted on collecting the taxes, arrears and fines, they were fed fish pies stuffed with poisonous vegetables. Two of them became insane, were driven into the woods and left to perish there. The third one, a Jew, was tortured and cast into the river.

No commissar ever ventured into the village after that. Those who were sent (much as an Oriental potentate might send an official in disfavor into a lion's den), pretended sickness, or insanity. Besides, the general status of the Soviets was precarious at the time; the fall of the Bolsheviki was said to be imminent. Thus, in spite of persistent rumors that a punitive expedition would be sent against the community of murderers, the villagers pursued their amusing pranks, confident that they were immune in their white impenetrable plains.

As soon as the Revolution broke out they rushed to the estate of Protopopov, millionaire and eccentric, pillaged and sacked his priceless treasure, killed the precious prize-cows and bulls and had a barbecue at which the poor landlord's presence was humbly requested at the point of a carver previously used in slaughtering the cattle. Every moujik brought a barrel of his own brand of home brew and all, men, women, and children, drank and made merry. Even dogs lapped up the puddles of vodka and later could be seen reeling through the unpaved streets. The feast over, they impaled the landowner and carried his dead body through the village. When an elderly peasant remonstrated with them for their wicked deeds and reminded them of a variety of infernal punishment in store for them, they took a pot of boiling pitch, smeared it over his mouth and pasted his beard and mustache together, as if anxious to definitely rid themselves of his further gibbering. The efforts of the unfortunate fellow to open his mouth were of no avail. His eyes bulged, the veins on his forehead fairly burst. And being asthmatic, the man could not stand the strain; he died from a heart attack. The villagers washed his face, scraped off the pitch, and gave him a lavish burial.

During the tragic days of famine and blockade, aggravated by an almost uninterrupted period of rain, when the few paths leading to the village had turned into impassable welter, the villagers took to cannibalism for a while. The valiant fight with their consciences, before deciding to grind the axe and publicly slaughter the first meal-provider, was probably the only glimpse of moral courage in the lives of these reprobates. The pangs of hunger were unbearable. There was not a grain in the village, and Pakhom, the chief, had ordered the casting of lots to determine who should be eaten first. The details of their first meal were related to Vladi by Osya, the tavern-keeper, whose wares consisted of *baranki*, dry age-old doughnuts, home brew, and roast pork at least a month old.

"God will have to forgive us," he spoke, "because it was His own fault. That's the way I figured it out with the notary. If He didn't want us to commit crimes, He could have stopped the famine easily enough, couldn't He? Isn't He omnipotent? Well, He didn't. We hadn't eaten for three days. Hadn't even any rats. So that's how. We drew lots, and let me tell you a secret, it was Pakhom himself who drew the first lot, ha-ha! Lord!—maybe he didn't get pale! . . . He shook like an aspen. But the notary fixed it for him, and muddled the whole business. We feasted on Lusha—or was it Darya? We had only two such meals, and I don't recall who was eaten first?"

"What did it taste like?" Vladi asked, dumbfounded. The innkeeper's swinish face was round and sleek, and he thought at the time that he had smeared lard over it.

"Not bad at all," he answered readily, as if the taste of that gruesome meal had been still in his mouth. "Sort of sweetish, like horse meat. Others say it was like crab meat, but I never ate crabs. I couldn't ever get myself to eat such froggy stuff. The French, they say, eat frogs, and other such mammals. Tfoo—oo!" And he spat aside.

Fortunately the roads had frozen and a number of peasants in sleighs ventured out onto the highway. Right near the city they waylaid a few itinerant merchants, and procured provisions for the village. The curious part of it all was the fact that several women insisted on continuing the cannibalistic practice even after food had become plentiful in the village. Two women decoyed a fat peasant into the bath and tried to cut him up into steak. His screams attracted one of the midgets who happened to be passing and who joined the victim in his lusty cries for help! The latter was saved, not without some damage to his envied corpulence. He lost both ear lobes regarded as rare delicacies by those versed in the edibility of human flesh; they tasted not unlike highly prized cockscombs. Pakhom severely punished the women, and had them each work three months in the victim's yard, as they were in no position to offer financial indemnity.

There were other incidents to enliven those monotonous, post-revolutionary days in the village, and these were related to Vladi by Lidda, the vixenish girl in whose hut he had been quartered, and who watched his every step, like a kitten. One of the episodes concerned her directly. She was the illegitimate daughter of the immensely rich landowner Protopopov, whose land holdings aggregated thousands of acres. The landowner's lasciviousness was a matter of common knowledge. He recognized no law—human or divine—and was not averse to increasing the size of families wherever he chanced to sojourn for a few days. He seemed to have taken a strange liking to Lidda, or Lidka (as the pale little girl was called)—a fancy that was far from being purely paternal. Fortunately for Lidda, his frightful death put an end to his amorous designs.

Lidka's mother was a plain peasant woman; but somehow nature had endowed her with intelligence and fine tact. Perhaps this was why the landowner was so uncommonly fond of her and her child, and had Lidka reared in a truly bourgeois fashion; he even sent a governess from Paris into the swamps of the *tundra* region. Peasant women were green with envy, and children of the village would hiss the hideous word *baystrook* (bastard) whenever Lidka passed them. Their invectives became so virulent that, in time, the girl never left the palatial home built by her father. There, like the princess Tamara in her high tower on the Georgian cliffs, she lived; like a hothouse flower, like a weird orchid transplanted with utmost care from exotic lands into the dreary frozen, snow-covered plains of the North, swaying on its stem, undecided whether it wants to live and dream of its hot native soil, or to die and thus forgo a life of misery.

After the tragic death of her father, which she was forced to witness; after the shameful treatment which the peasants accorded the governess—they made her drink vodka and eat herrings and sing French songs—it was on her that the villagers centred their attention. She kept silent and faced the brutal hooligans with haughty contempt. They left her unharmed. After all, she was one of them, a child of a peasant woman whom they all knew and who would have been with them right now to enjoy all the benefits of the newly won liberties, had she not been killed in a storm by a falling tree. And the girl, too, was a child of the North, one of them. They felt her contemptuous look on them, but decided it would not be fair to harm her.

"Let her stay with us," someone suggested.

"Let her know the peasant's lot," another added.

"But no high towers, no turrets nor castles for her," was the warning of an old woman.

"That is understood," still another exclaimed. "Now that we are all equal, we are going to occupy that big house in turn."

Subsequently they confiscated her good clothes and finery and gave her coarse, rough, homespun linen and hemp garments. She was forced to move to her aunt's, her mother's older sister, a poor wretch living from hand to mouth.

For a while she was left alone. Presently the women of the village began to claim that, for her past years of leisure, she owed them some kind of service. Lidka was compelled to chop wood, carry water, and feed the pigs for several families. All this she did, with a haughty grin; only her eyes burned all the while with a malicious fire that would frighten anyone but the Northern women of that accursed village. For they all had the making of witches, and nothing could frighten them. Some of them even participated in bear-hunting, like Amazons.

And so they had been driven into this bizarre village which is not recorded even on official maps, their course prescribed by the fatal encounter with the negro. Like a tipsy African potentate the negro crouched on the litter, almost delighted at the fear his imposing body instilled in a group of women on the outskirts of the village. Presently they were brought before the starshina, the mayor of the village, a giant with a shaggy red beard. Some of the men tried to lift Tom's hair thinking it a hair-dress or a wig.

"Karakul," a moujik remarked with a wicked smile.

Another moujik rubbed Tom's skin with a currycomb in the hope of rubbing the black off and bringing the more natural white to the surface. He was stupefied at the failure of his efforts.

"Devil himself," he mumbled in bewilderment. "Where did you pick him up, Christian folk?"

The peasants were delighted to hear that the three men were actors and acrobats. The whole village was agog with the anticipation of a gala festival, The bells rang, children shouted, dogs barked: the villagers were ready for the first theatrical performance in the history of the village. In view of the condition of the negro's foot, the performance had to be postponed.

In half an hour the operation was performed. Two villagers held the negro, and the theology student, with one deft swing of his carver, severed the leg. With a soft rustle it fell in the deep snow.

Later in the evening he found out that Tom was resting comfortably. He paid him a visit. The negro bitterly complained of the women. They simply would not let him sleep, intent upon establishing whether the man was entirely chocolate-colored.

He chased the women away, and asked Lidda to stay with the negro and be his nurse for a while. He had noticed her strikingly pale, noble face in that ragged crowd, as an eager connoisseur notices a small dusty masterpiece amidst a hundred and one paintings at the auctioneer's. And yet she looked humble, seemingly afraid to be too much in the eyes of the villagers. Even her gait was lithe, as if she touched the ground with revulsion, the same ground on which so many foul toes had left their imprint. . . .

She left all his questions unanswered, limiting herself to a quick nod, a curt monosyllable, or an imperative gesture. He did not mind her aloofness in the least. She fascinated him. Whether it was her mystic paleness or the haughty gleam in her eyes, he did not know. Her supple body was so flexible that at times it seemed she could touch her toes with her incredibly red lips.

Once he saw her near the well. The day was not as cold as usual, and she wore no kerchief. He noticed how thick and glossy her hair was, how beautifully she braided it.

"You are always silent, Ariadne," he said. She laughed.

"What did you call me?" she asked.

"I said you were always silent," he replied, stupefied.

"No, no," she exclaimed. "You called me Ariadne."

"Did I?" he asked her sheepishly. All the time he kept staring at her. For the first time it occurred to him that she was a perfect image of Ariadne, the one he had lost forever in the streets of Moscow. Not that she looked like her. She was taller, her eyes were bigger, and her face was more pallid. But at that moment, near the well, he attributed the change to the fact that she had grown; that she most likely was not a reality but a vision; and that she would soon vanish as swiftly as she had come once again into his life. But her smile, her demeanor, her gait, her tresses, her red lips were all Ariadne's.

When he turned to her—she no longer was at the well. Far away, in the cabin of Pakhom she was, and he caught himself saying: "Ariadne, are you really here?"

THE very first week of their stay in that strange village he made a determined attempt to flee. Not because every face was brutal and criminal; not because of the unrelieved dreariness of that forsaken hole; but because three quarters of the villagers were diseased.

They were treated like outlandish toys. Indeed, when not forced to perform, they enjoyed as much liberty as the rest of the villagers. Yet, wherever he went, he felt the spying eyes of the natives. God knows why these wanted them to stay; perhaps it was the labour they did; perhaps their circus tricks which the villagers had never seen before. For the village was absolutely inaccessible both in summer, when the swamps surrounded it with engulfing vapors, and in winter, when townsfolk would not venture into it for fear of murder and rapine. No more than five or ten craftsmen left for town every winter, disregarding swamps and wolves, and returned home in the Spring with some money, rusks, brandy, and the horrid disease whose symptoms they would notice only when it was too late to be cured, and when their tonsils were red and all diseased.

In one hut he found a whole family of eight in the throes of this death-breathing disease, slowly rotting away. The man had brought it from town, and transmitted it to his wife; from her it passed on to her lover, who happened to live in the same shack with them. The children, one after another, became sick. No one paid attention to their ghastly appearance.

"If they die we'll bury them," Pakhom said. "We'll all die some day."

And the notary added: "As is shown by statistics on the interrelations of society and various interests, so to speak, the members . . ."

As usual, he could not find his way to the main clause, and left the whole phrase unfinished.

"However, we meet in the hall soon, and you show your tricks!" Pakhom said with satisfaction. "A good time will be had by all."

His first attempt to flee was made after he had seen a half-decayed woman with a child in her arms. The child's face was surly, wrinkled, and idiotic, covered with blotches and pimples.

"Why don't you take it to the hospital?" he asked, standing as far away from her as he could.

"The hospital is too far," she said with resignation. Her voice was hoarse, and she frequently sniffed when she spoke, as if she had a severe cold. There she stood, an ancient wizened mummy with a smaller mummy in her ghastly arms. Then her husband crept forth. He could not walk straight, and when he spoke, superhuman cruelty flickered in his narrow eyes.

Instinctively he wended his steps to the outskirts of the village. The hardships of a desperate plunge back to the wilderness were almost romantically alluring when he thought that he was about to leave forever that stupendous conglomeration of derelicts. There was a strange significance in the fact that he had to go through such a purgatory to reach Ariadne. The bestiality of the villagers was beyond description. The very first day of their arrival, in a brawl over the paltry sum of a hundred roubles a man killed another by slashing his throat with a cobbler's knife and grabbing the money. The victim was buried, and the murderer had to return the money to the widow and do penance for a month until the *starshina* should decide how big a fine he would pay to the village. . . .

But as he was about to slip out of the village, he felt the pressure of a hand on his shoulder. He gave a start. In the twilight he saw a man with a dirty kerchief wound across his face to cover the gaping hole where once there had been a nose. He jumped aside and rushed back into the village.

He had become almost reconciled to the thought of living in the diseased village, when he made another discovery: there were at least a dozen hermaphrodites in the place, half of them midgets, inoffensive, but grotesquely ugly. Their faces were yellow and sallow, fat, round, inexpressive. Even their chinks of eyes seemed to be yellow, like thin slits made in old parchment.

They spoke in piping, whimpering voices, tremulous and whining like the screeching of an ungreased wheel. The sight of a barren hermaphrodite always made him tremble with curiosity: whether because he did not consider it a human being, or because of acute envy of its complete victory over all the sexual troubles that harass man's soul. He watched them with intense curiosity, as if he might learn from them that supreme unattainable art of suppressing excruciating complexes.

The midgets, especially, were dreadful. Never before had he seen creatures quite like them. His first experience with one of them was so horrid that he swooned. It was the second or third day after he had drifted into the village. The old woman slept soundly. Unable to conjure up sleep he sat on the bench. There was no one in the shack. Suddenly the door opened. He thought it was Lidda, and made a motion to rise, when suddenly someone struck a match and he caught the glimpse of a ghostly face, very old and shrivelled, not more than three feet above the ground. His voice froze in his throat, his body disappeared, as if it had merged with the dusk. But the vision lasted for a moment only. Soon all was darkness again—and that was the most horrid part of it. He was so exhausted with fear and emotion that he could not get down to light the wood-splinter, that chandelier of the Russian village. His eyes were closed. Yet somehow he felt that the ghost had not disappeared, but was slowly creeping to his side guided by his own phosphorescence. Indeed, soon some one touched him and giggled.

The giggle was all he heard. He screamed and fainted. The hut was dark and quiet as if nothing had happened. As soon as he regained the mastery of his voice he began suddenly to shout with such piercing shrillness that soon Lidda and Atma rushed in.

"That was no ghost," Lidda exclaimed when he told her what he had seen. "That was Kirilla, the midget. He won't do you any harm."

And indeed, they never did him any harm. Later on he saw the same Kirilla who had scared him so. He had a big head, a diminutive body, and very short arms. He ran after him and shouted: "Come, play with us, you good man!" He ran away from him. He could not look into his leonine face. Later on, however, he became accustomed to them, and even permitted them to peep over his shoulders as he wrote down his musical thoughts.

Not all of the hermaphrodites were cretins or midgets. Two or three of them showed keen judgment, and as keen a cruelty as the rest; they were very big, very stout, very round; and with thinly disguised contempt looked down on the villagers. One of them was a follower of the *skoptzi* sect, the sect that with the view of accelerating the Millennium advocates emasculation of men and cessation of all birth. He was an ardent propagandist, and during their stay in the village there were two conversions. It was so dreadful a sight that it is impossible to speak here of the ceremony.

But gradually he became accustomed to the ways of this stupendous village; though ofttimes, when it occurred to him that in his daily intercourse he might have been touched by this or that syphilitic, he rushed to the yard thickly covered with snow, and wallowed in its immaculate whiteness, moaning with repugnance, as if eager to purify his very breath with the chastity of undefiled snow. Avidly he inhaled the icy air whose elemental currents were ever changing, ever purifying themselves with regenerated freshness which alone could bring relief to his sickened heart.

But slowly repugnance and fear left his soul and he began to disregard the incredible horror of that weird place. Indifference crept into his mind and the everyday routine brought dulling but salutary relief. In time he failed to be aroused even by the hottentotish customs of the villagers and their insane jokes. It was the blissful resignation of the Andante of the Fifth Symphony, after the trembling fingers pointing to heaven have become helplessly limp, after the fruitless challenge has spent itself in a vain attempt to capture and hold on to the illusory semblance of a star that trembles with a knowing coldness and the mocking certainty of unassailability. Sweet and sad are the harmonies, and yet nothing has been captured, nothing has been said or defined and no decision reached in spite of the ever recurring wail of the flute that stubbornly and grimly pierces the increasing dusk. And thus shall it remain forever for men to speak, and sing, and lament and writhe in agony and admire their own death and wipe their own helpless tears.

Now Ariadne was with him, and the miraculously found violin spoke in divine accents, subduing and overshadowing all other voices.

Ere long they became full-fledged members of that strange community. The danger of being beaten, or eaten, or tarred and feathered had passed. They supplied the missing element of theatricality. Tom, whose leg had healed in due course of time, juggled balls and sang negro songs. Atma hissed and roared his incantations, twirling in wild contortions, stabbing himself cruelly until he bled, and throwing the whole meeting into a paroxysm of madness. The women tore off their garments, exposed their bodies, and moaned in wild ecstasy.

Vladi's share in entertaining them was to play an old violin picked up in the landowner's mansion. The sounds of the old Italian instrument hovered in the huge hall of the mansion where once nobility used to assemble. The peasants listened with amazement to the melodies they had never before heard.

"No man in the world can play as beautifully as you," the notary said. "It's, I should say, simply mnemonical."

The crowd yelled: "That was well said!"

After the concert—never before—supper consisting of cabbage soup and lard was served. Tom moaned, gnashed his teeth, and cursed at the lack of variety in food. But he ate just the same. He ate very much, and grew fatter every day. But even his voraciousness was not held against him. The villagers still retained their somewhat worshipful attitude toward him. Whenever he hobbled by, they crossed themselves. The older peasants maintained that the negro was a forerunner of the Antichrist "as is foretold in the Book of Wisdom of Isac of Sirach, that black Ethiopians with tails hidden in their entrails so as to fool mankind will appear on earth and prepare the world for the last judgment and the trumpets of Gabriel." The more inquisitive peasants even tried to make sure whether there were no visible traces of a tail appended to his body. He complained to Pakhom and the quest of the tail had to be discontinued.

The nights were dreadfully long. He could not sleep. Atma—they were quartered together—urged him to join him and flee the village. But when he thought of the big one-legged negro, he was seized with a great pity. He pictured him alone, a black helicopter on the barren white surface of the Northern wilderness, jumping to salvation. He would never find his way to Arkhangel, and so he would be forced to remain in this village, which in the summer was completely surrounded by malaria-breeding swamps and cut off from the rest of the world. He pictured him married and breeding mulattoes and growing fatter every day, as if the ever-present vitality of the sawed-off leg sought an even distribution over the rest of the body.

He refused to flee. Soon he would become an integral part of this devastating North, and his body, and all the melodies it bore, would dissolve tracelessly into the elemental swamps. The sounds would roam like orphans, unconjured by the feverish yearnings of a creative soul. At night they would drift over the roofs of the decaying shacks, and the dogs would howl in mortal agony. And one girlish soul would sob and pine away. He had fallen to such low depths that at night, when his mind was feverishly at work, he wrung his fingers with terror at the mere thought of his degeneracy. And when he turned to Ariadne and the cadence of her speech, now irretrievably lost in the cold past of mankind, he groaned and wiped his quivering eyelids. Behind these shadows, in the impenetrable thicket, her spectre glistened, the unattainable one whom he had wed in his heart and whom he had never ceased to worship. Under the Septentrional skies studded with stars, he evoked figure after figure from different worlds, as if he needed the supporting background for her flimsy vision; and Parrel busily instructed the negro, and suddenly Ladislas Lerner began to lecture to the midgets on the charm of well-paid Hebrew music.

A warm breath hovered over him. It was Lidda. He searched for her face, and pressed his lips against hers. She did not resist. But when he became too bold, she firmly said: "Be quiet, or you'll be sorry."

"You're driving me mad," he suddenly said. "Ariadne, Ariadne!"

"What a strange name," she exclaimed, stroking his beard. "You are great. You are strong. Your eyes shine when you play. . . . Now kiss me, kiss me with all the fire of your heart. But don't attempt to do me any violence. I imagine that in your heart there is still a spark of true love for me."

"More than that, Ariadne!" he whispered. She was the illusion of his illusion, and love was nothing else but that: the reflection of a definite image drawn somewhere, somehow, perhaps in another existence.

"You'll take me away from here," she said. "I'll go with you wherever you go. We'll stop at market places, you'll play and I'll sing. I have a lovely voice."

They spoke for hours, and again their love, the shadowy substance of life—at least as real as life and as vague in its bliss—sang in them to the accompaniment of two lone voices enhanced by all the misunderstandings of introspection. Like two mirrors between which nothing has been placed and then reflected a million times with all the alluring details of a perfect void, their souls peered into each other. Each spoke of a thousand things, and the other read a thousand new things into them, as lovely; until, like an avalanche, their sudden passion rolled into their hearts and made them gaze into each other's eyes with flaming curiosity.

THEIR captivity would have, probably, lasted eternally, if it had not been for the negro.

As said, the villagers considered him an imp, and did everything in their power to placate his latent malevolence. As time wore on, they became more indifferent, especially after their request for a successful hunting expedition had not been granted in spite of his exorcisms and prayers. The negro's prestige was on the wane. Further severe tests proved beyond reasonable doubt that he was just an ordinary human being even if off color.

The death of a horse and two cows definitely established the overwhelming guilt of the negro. Pakhom and his retinue invaded the hut and without much ado tied and bound the negro, and threw him on the table, a helpless cargo frozen with horror. He spluttered, and shrieked, and cursed, and even made an attempt to bite someone's inadvertently near finger. They were inexorable, and the theology student made three deep incisions in his body, then dragged it with them. In this way they tried out the force of the evil spirit. If the negro should die before the cock's crow, he would be considered innocent and absolved, for at that time the evil spirits would leave his body and join hell. If he should keep on living, then they would have to kill him, for that would be a sure indication that he was possessed and that the devil in him was strong enough not to be afraid to roam even in daylight.

A dreadful calm settled over the village. Night held her magic sway in the fantastically white streets. No doubt the villagers were afraid to show up where the devil was waging a desperate fight. Unable to stand the agony, Vladi left the hut and crept to the church.

The moon cast her white light, and he glided from shack to shack, along the slumbering oak walls. Not a voice to be heard, not a face to be seen in the windows. Even the dogs were dreadfully silent.

He reached the wooden church, clutching the bottle of water in his hand. The moon hid behind a cloud, and he stole in.

A faint groan reached his ear. The negro lay before the pulpit, twisted like a caterpillar crushed by a heavy boot. His face was ashen; he literally swam in a puddle of blood.

"Do you hear me?" Vladi asked, ungagging him.

"I am thirsty," he whispered. "Brother, my brother, save me!"

He drank all the water in the bottle. "Who are you?" he asked then. "Are they going to murder me?"

"No, no," Vladi exclaimed.

The negro opened his eyes, and spoke less feverishly.

"Ah, that's you!" He at last recognized him. "Oh, it hurts . . . This wound, and that, and another, here and there. And when you want water, your lips touch the cold floor . . . Wait, some day I'll have all Russia burned, and the ashes on an ash-tray with a really stinking stogie . . . What do you think of that?"

"Calm yourself," Vladi sadly said. "We're trying to save you."

"I've got something that may save me yet," the negro suddenly said. "But you must swear that you won't double-cross me."

"I'll swear all right," Vladi assured him.

"I've got a few diamonds hid in the left corner of my cabin," Tom quickly whispered, and Vladi recalled with what care the negro had held on to the hem of his trousers. They probably had contained the treasure which he later thought safer to entrust to the ground.

"Give 'em one stone," the negro whispered. "They's fifteen together. You hear? I'm half dead. . . ."

He found the stones imbedded in clay, under a heavy board. Without much delay he repaired to the house of the notary, the greediest and vainest of them all, and made the bid for the negro's freedom. The scribe cursed and swore and rubbed his gummed eyes—it was long past midnight—until his sleepy eyes fell on the sparkling stone with an almost amorous tenderness. He was ready to help the poor man.

"But," he said with an ingratiating smile, "you must promise me to keep silent and pay no attention to whatever happens to-morrow, for I may have to resort to some odd tricks to save the poor lonely negro, who must be so lonely without a fleshy cocoanut!"

"Very well," Vladi said, handing him the stone on which the beams of the moon played in a most miraculous fashion. "But remember, if you don't stick to your promise, you'll regret it."

He disregarded the threat and solemnly said: "I'll have to draw on all my resourcefulness to save the poor chocolate fellow. Don't worry and don't be excruciated by the pangs of spiritual torments, for, plot as they may, the black life of this Ethiopian microcosmos will be unequivocally spared in the name of salutary humanitarianism and for future reference. Tolstoy, for instance. . . ."

Indeed, next day extraordinary events wended their course in a grotesque succession.

Several hours passed in agony,—neither he nor Atma was allowed to leave the hut. Soon Lidda came and put an end to their anxiety. The original plan of boiling the negro alive had been abandoned, and it had been decided to banish him to the forest. The notary had made an eloquent plea, invoking "the well known placidity of the international law, which, so to say is the category of the universal." It was this stirring plea that led the villagers to spare the negro's life, much to the disappointment of the women, who cast sad glances at the huge shining cauldron and the big wood pile towering in front of the church: all the details of the exciting ceremony had been so carefully planned and the spectacle would really be unforgettable!

Now, since the boiling of the head-henchmen of the Antichrist had been given up, the women began to prick him with forks and sharp-edged sticks. He could barely hop about, painfully at a loss to account for the villagers' attitude. He zigzagged on his solitary leg, helpless, ridiculous. The peasants stood round him, staring at him with a morbid curiosity in their quizzical eyes, not unlike children watching the agony of a fly deprived of wings and legs.

Soon the circle of peasants began to close on him. The whole village was out, crowds milled about with a solemnity that was almost pathetic in its aimlessness. The day was superb. The winter sun shone with all the resplendence of a benevolent planet. The oak facades of the log cabins were blue in shadow, and equally blue were their weird shadows on the snow. All the faces had suddenly acquired an orange tint extremely pleasant to the eye.

On that day the negro was driven to the forest. Several boys with Kirila, the midget, were left to keep the outcast from returning home.

S HE was at his side. With her came the bracing freshness of a crisp evening. There was the peculiar tang of virgin forests in her thick black tresses, the charm of a Septentrional night in her blue eyes. Everything about her, even the hypnotic attraction of normal perspiration suggestive of vigorous beauty, made his heart throb. Her serpentine body bent over him, and with her chapped fingers she rumpled his hair. He strained her to him. Her cheek touched his, her fingers sought his with the clasp of feverish amity. He slipped his arms round her, but she eluded his embrace with the slipperiness of a young seal.

In the darkness the two Ariadnes now merged forever. The forms of their bodies crumbled under his prying eye, and the more he sought to sever them the more stubbornly they clung to each other, now one and inseparable. The illusion was complete, like the circle in wake of a pebble tossed on the surface of a lake. He loved her with the sustained pathos of accepted and satisfied love. A meditative somnolence held him spellbound. This was his land, his home, and the eternal abode of his beloved. And even from the purgatory of the village, from the insane antics of the midgets, from the howling wind and blinding *purgah* he would draw the grotesque background for his new symphony.

Like a grey shadow she crouched in the corner. He picked up the violin and patted its slender neck and the graceful body throbbing under his fingers. It seemed as though the very touch of human flesh made it resound with an infinity of unknown melodies. Every time he took it into his hands, his heart palpitated, as if he had come face to face with Ariadne afloat in the blue lagoon. By what strange fortunes, through what unknown seas and glamorous ports had it passed to reach this marshy wilderness? Perhaps a Sicilian prince had bought it from Stradivarius himself and presented it to a fabulously rich Muscovite potentate, who sent it for safekeeping into his Northern stronghold, where some day one of his illegitimate sons might play upon it. And thus it had hung in the cellar for two centuries, until the villagers had forced open the most jealously guarded treasures of the landlord's castle and brought it to light. To them it must have seemed unimportant as compared with the more appreciable wines and liqueurs.

Now it was his, the priceless soul of an Italian genius, suffused with his own candid spirit. No sooner had he touched the strings than he became transported into strange places. Exotic faces surrounded him. Through lakes and dales he swiftly flew, and once again he was back in New York, once again he attacked the strings and evoked the Mendelssohn Concerto and her slender figure on the causette. Closer and closer she moved to him, until her breath enveloped him. Her eyes were cold and indifferent, and a huge rosary of autographed portraits of great musicians lay at her feet. Alongside of her lay Merrick Parrel, completely nude, hairy like a young ape, his huge wrists twisted around her body. The orchestral strains of the violaxophiano quivered in the Studio, and she whispered condescendingly: "I am almost amused."

He played Bach's Chaconne, in vain trying to find Ariadne's luminous eyes in the squalid hut, now drowned in the mystic beauty of darkness. The melody was endless like hunger, and the famished soul of the instrument spoke of hope and peace. Somewhere in the dark hut the degenerate face of Parrel grinned eerily. It was a different world, the one he had left behind, the one he might never join again, the eternal squabbling of the musical coteries in New York, the market values of musical wares, and the last scene of his on earth—the evening with Ariadne, nude and teasing—now flickered by in a rapid succession.

All about him darkness prevailed, and only the ghostly face of Atma stared at him. In the darkness she crept over to his side. He hung the violin, and she held his hand, and brought his face near to hers. Her eyes shone with unrestrained tears. Not in vain had he braved two courts-martial, not in vain had he roamed through deserts and oceans! Here this girl had been waiting for him, while her lovely image played havoc with his illusions amassed on the other half of the globe.

He seized her arms, and blurted out mad words in English, in all the queer English he then recalled. She was frightened, but silent. He sobbed feverishly. Ariadne, beloved child of the obscure band-leader! How did she ever get here? At last, after months of endless toil and heartache he had found her. He made a superhuman effort to refrain from strangling her, for he had the morbid desire to test her material substance, as if he were distrusting his senses. She was quivering in his arms. At last, overcome by the sheer impact of his agitation, he grew calm and laid his hands on her head.

"How I love you!" he moaned. "God alone reads my heart."

"Some day I may love, you, if . . . if we ever get out of this dirty hole where the sun shuns us with jeering malice for three quarters of the year. Look at my fingers! They are chapped, and rough from eternal dipping into icy water and peeling of frozen potatoes . . . Oh, how I hate these bearded Asiatics! How many times have they tried to attack me! . . ."

"Ariadne, Ariadne!"

"Why do you repeat that word? What is Ariadne?" she asked in amazement.

"You must let me call you Ariadne," he implored. "That's an American name. After we have made our getaway we'll go to New York together. That is, that always has been your home. You must get used to being called by that beautiful name Ariadne!"

"Ariadne, Ariadne," she repeated, and he quivered as the shadows of the past swept by in their ever sharp outlines. He placed her on his knees, and caressed her tresses. She was as calm as a forest before a storm. When he lifted her, mad with desire, and carried her to the whitewashed bunk near the oven, she bit his ear and slid down.

"You aren't going to do me any harm," she said ironically. "Stronger men than you have tried to attack me and failed. Once, three moujiks, including a butcher followed me into a barn. They manhandled and nearly choked me. But God saved me. I never left this hut without a supply of well ground pepper. This I blew in their eyes, and while they were roaring with pain, I shoved myself through a hole in the wall and fled like a goat through the cold night. Finally I reached the house of Pakhom, and sobbed out my story to him. The three men were severely beaten, and after that I was not molested. Not because they believed in justice, these lice, but simply because they are jealous of one another . . . Ah, they are envious, these primitive cavemen! Some day I may like you, but if you ever lay your hands on me, I'll never see you again."

But all through the nocturnal hours he thought he heard her purring: "I'm pretty, oh, I'm pretty, and Ariadne is my name . . . I'm much prettier than I look, for I stoop when I walk, I am dirty and don't dress, afraid to excite the lust of these brutal rustics who are like vermin . . . Even some of the hermaphroditic midgets are after me. They scheme and set traps to possess my virgin flesh! Isn't that queer? . . ."

Like Carmen, she hurled her Tra-la-la into his face and seemed quieted for the rest of the night. Presently, the old woman came in, lit the oil-soaked splinter and, without removing her clothes, squatted in the corner and fell asleep.

"Why don't *you* undress?" came Ariadne's voice. "I want to undress, too."

She ordered him to go to sleep. He put the light out, and heard the magic rustle of her coarse garment falling to the floor. So dazzlingly white was her naked body that he saw its outlines in the impenetrable darkness, as if she had borne an inner magic light to make her body transparent. His mind was troubled. It was beyond his strength to sleep in one room with her. He would have given half his life to have her lie near him, to stroke her hair, and whisper words of tenderness into her tiny ears.

Suddenly he felt a warm breath over him.

"If you'll be good and if you promise to behave, I'll lie near you, and we'll talk," she whispered.

"I will, Ariadne, I will, beloved," he replied. Soon her warm body, stripped of its coarse garb, lay near his. As there was not enough space for both of them on the narrow cot, they lay closely entwined as if their bodies were one. For a moment he thought he held, like Goethe's *Erlkoenig*, a small child in his arms, whom he was to carry through elfine regions. He kissed her with brotherly respect and cautious restraint, and she showed her appreciation by a faint pressure of her fingers.

Stroking his hair, warding off his erratic motions, she unburdened her soul. There were tears in her voice. She was tired of brutal feelings. All her life she had been fighting attackers. She had been first attacked when only fourteen years old. It was her dog that saved her then. Her own father, who came on a short visit to his vast domain, took a fancy to her and made various unequivocal advances. He had last seen her at the age of ten months; when he next came North, she was eighteen years. She fought his incestuous attempts with the ferocity of a wolverine. The revolution thwarted the landlord's ambitions; he was impaled by drunken peasants and his body, with its dangling intestines, was carried through the village like an ikon during a solemn ecclesiastical celebration. She was tremendously tired, little Lidda. She had been reared like a girl of the upper classes and was now enslaved by her former slaves, treated like a peasant outcast and watched at every step. She missed her piano and wanted to speak French. She longed to see refined faces. Her own piano had been used as fuel, and she herself was gradually brutalized. Soon she would join the ranks of the village Amazons.

She fell asleep, and he lay awake through the night, afraid to stir, afraid to awake his precious burden.

NEXT day the scribe disappeared. He had fled at night, and it was not until the next afternoon that his flight was definitely established. Ariadne, who knew what was in back of it, revealed the criminal selfishness of the scribe to the *starshina*.

The news spread like wildfire, and soon the whole village was buzzing with excitement. Summoned before Pakhom, Vladi corroborated the story told by Ariadne. Pakhom was trembling with rage.

"Two thousand roubles in gold!" he shouted. "That man will hang for it."

Almost all the male population was out with dogs and horses to take part in the man-hunt and share in the unexpected loot. Like cheap movie-villains, some peasants actually sharpened their knives. A few fierce looking viragoes joined in the preparations. Pakhom's last words were: "Hey, you, keep an eye on these two chaps, we'll soon be back."

But their plans for escape had already been worked out in detail. Ariadne waited for them with three horses near Pakhom's stable. They made ready to join her, but stifled with difficulty a shriek of despair: two women had entered and began to watch them. As time passed, he grew more and more desperate. He heard the familiar whistle of Ariadne. As they were not far from the stable, he suddenly pushed one of the women aside, and made a quick dash to the door. Atma followed him. Close upon their heels ran the two enraged women. But by the time these furies, and a few others whom their mad shouts had brought out of their lairs were at the stable,—they were ready to take off. He whipped the horse, and struck the woman with the whip. She screamed and fell.

They were now galloping full tilt out of the village. One of the midgets was not quick enough and Ariadne's horse crushed his skull.

The excitement in the village was beyond description. Everywhere they saw distorted faces, women, dwarfs, diseased recluses. Beside themselves with rage and envy, the women saddled their horses and doggedly plodded after them for hours.

Their horses were ugly, but marvellous runners, typical Northern stallions, with limitless endurance. They galloped two days and a night, stopping for a short while to give Ariadne a rest. And again they dashed through the marshy tundra.

Summer was in full swing, and the ground was moist with the muddy thawings of obdurate snow. Brown puddles flashed here and there. In some places the bare ground was visible, and now and then its drab nudity stared at them in stark ugliness.

At the end of the second day they heard the dull thud of hoofs behind. But right before them was the town of Solvichegodsk. They had nothing to fear. They could ride in and ask protection from the brutal assailers who still had to account for the murder of the tax-collector. And indeed, Pakhom, who always managed to keep his head cool, showed his tactfulness by inviting all to a *traktir* and drinking with a merry wink to the good health of Agafon, the scribe. A crowd of drab looking townspeople joined them at the counter.

When the villagers were ready to leave, Ariadne slipped a big bottle of whisky into the hands of Pakhom. With a strange flash of her huge grey eyes, she enjoined him to celebrate her new freedom.

Their captivity lasted one year.

They remained in the town a while to obtain funds needed for the last lap of their journey. The stones were worth a good deal; yet they had not the price of a loaf.

But somehow they managed to make ends meet. He played in the taverns. His music attracted big crowds. Whenever he played popular songs such as The Poor Chap Died in the Military Hospital, or I'll Recognize My Sweetie by His Gait, they all wept and threw small coins in Ariadne's hat. For even though their poverty was great and money scarce, they were sentimental, and always ready to shed tears.

THEY were about to leave the village and make a dash for the frontier, when he suddenly became aware of a lovely boy following them with his large melancholy eyes. Wherever they went they saw him, always in the company of an old man.

In the evening, tired after the day's tramp, they entered their tavern, ordered tea and rusks, and sat in the corner, silent and meditative. A year had passed since he had left the other world. Now he had the deadening certainty of being surrounded by merciless enemies. He quivered, and lightly pressed Ariadne's hand under the table. She looked at him with inexplicable sadness, letting her limp palm rest in his.

The old man, tipsy and tottering, broke a tumbler, and they hastily helped him out of the dive, past the infuriated barkeep. The boy thanked them in his melodious voice. Like Ganymede he was, except for the ugly scar on his forehead, hidden under his high fur cap. Supplicatingly his lovely eyes rested on them. His girlish face was pale with emotion, his nostrils dilated, as he turned to Ariadne, who seemed unable to take her eyes off his angelic face.

Atma helped the old man, now suddenly sober and morose, to his feet, and they followed both to the market place. The boy hid his face in his tattered muffler, like a grey marabout. Two men passed by. Their eyes seemed wicked and relentless. Night was falling. The men brushed by, lingering for a while and arrogantly eyeing Ariadne. Then they disappeared behind the corner of the shack, dreamily blue against a yellow horizon. As the boy quickly moved onward, they stuck their ominous heads from behind the wall and craned their necks.

"I fear them," he whispered. "Oh, Lord, how I fear them," he sobbed, and instinctively snuggled between them. Quite unconsciously they pressed their bodies tighter and almost carried him past the searching eyes beneath the high fur caps. Yet all the steps they took did not seem to diminish the distance, as if these eyes had enchained them.

Suddenly a plaintive sound, a sob, a sigh cut into the silence. The boy gave a start. A string had burst.

"Did you see those two men?" the boy hastily said. "They're after me. I know they're after me. Leave me, I beseech you, leave me, for we shall all perish."

"Let's go back. Let's go. What's your name?"

"Alexey."

"Alexey?" she repeated, as if trying to recall something.

"It's getting dark. Let me hold on to you."

"Yes, Alyosha. Never fear."

"I have seen horrors, I have seen horror upon horror," he whispered. "Again those two men. God . . . Cover me . . . Cover me . . . Thus . . . My heart ceased beating. Did you ever see a cave . . . full of rats . . . hands . . .

pale, long, hooked, nailed, stretched out to reach after your marrow. Pale, almost shining in the darkness. Then piles of human flesh, and you underneath. . . ."

They rushed past the two men. They merged with the night.

"Stop!" A sudden shriek. The blood froze in their veins. An icy squeak in the night. They stopped, rooted to the ground.

Like medallions, two unshaven faces hung in the darkness above the lantern. Narrow, triumphant, cold eyes, sure fingers.

"Passports . . ."

They scrutinized every word, they touched Ariadne's arms, they fixed queer glances upon the pale boy. The one with the big wart on the tip of his nose (all such men are cowards and liars) seized Ariadne's breasts and laughed.

"I thought you carried a gun." He laughed again, but a blaze of canine lust leered in his detestable eyes.

"The boy isn't your son, is he?" he asked.

"No," she scornfully retorted. "We're travelling musicians."

"I see," he drawled. "What kind of instrument do you hide here?" he asked, feeling her thighs and hips. His licentious hand travelled libidinously over her trembling limbs.

Soon they were alone. The two men had vanished in

the darkness, between God knows what stifling close walls. The boy seized Ariadne's hand.

"I shall never forget what you have done for me . . . The world will not forget it. How kind your eyes are, and how sterling your hearts . . . But don't leave me now, take me back to the tavern. We are still being shadowed."

He rose on his tiptoes and whispered: "Like a dream it was."

"But who are you?" she exclaimed.

They hurried through the deserted streets.

"Who are you, my boy? I swear to you we have no hand in this tragic chaos, nor do we understand it. Stay with us, it will be safer for you," Vladi begged.

They ran into the yard.

"No," the boy said resolutely. "I must go into the night at once, like a tracked beast. I am afraid of those two men. Have you ever lain under seven corpses, for a whole night, afraid to budge, on the verge of death? Have you ever been thrown on top of a scrap-heap of human flesh, bodies that were dear, inexplicably dear to you only a minute before? . . ."

"But who are you?" Vladi whispered.

Complete darkness enshrouded them. Dim candlelight filtered through a slit in the shutter.

"Can you see that strip of light? Someone is calling me. The Cheka is on our trail."

"But who are you?"

And he thought it was the wind that brought the answer—so faint, so incredible, so ghostly it was.

"I am Alexey, the Tsarevich."

"I knew it was you," Ariadne fervently said, pressing his palm. "I had known it all the while."

"Good-bye forever, and remember me, as I shall remember you," he said, and disappeared in the yard. The door screeched thinly.

Soon the dim light no longer rent the night with its burning blade.

"Another dream," he said.

"Another," she repeated.

"Is it a dream?"

"Is it?"

The moon appeared and faintly illumined the way. Atma slept soundly in the corridor, barring entrance to the world without. He lifted Ariadne and stepped over the body. She undressed in the darkness, and threw her clothes on the bunk.

"I am afraid of those two men," she whispered, slipping under the quilt. "Where are you, Vladi, where are you?"

Her arms sought him in the darkness.

"Here, here, my child, my love, my only one," he answered, and found her searching arms, and drew her flaming lips to his. She swung her arms around him, she clung to him frantically and spoke of sudden and unaccountable fears, weird apparitions, repellent faces she had once seen as a child; casual dreams that later had been mistaken for past and blunted realities. All the while her body throbbed like a butterfly flapping at the windowpane.

"Tell me, is it a dream?" she asked, kissing his eyes, mouth, forehead. "Do you recall the Tsarevich's eyes? Huge, round, mournful . . . you really think he is the Tsarevich?"

"I don't think so . . . The Tsar's entire family was executed in Ekaterinburg."

"No, no, no," she persisted like a child denied the moon. She was strangely restless, and she kissed him avidly as if she were never to see him again. "I want you to love me, to love me forever," she exclaimed, and burst out sobbing. Her body shook convulsively with passionate grief, and thus she grew calm in his arms, and became his wife.

All through the night they were awake, in the grip of a delirium of insatiable passion, as if she had felt, as if both of them had a vague premonition of what would happen on the morrow.

ARLY in the morning Ariadne, like an eel, slipped from beneath the blanket. She was nude and trembled from the matutinal chill. She hastened to unfasten one of the shutters and in the sudden play of Northern sunshine her lithe body suggested a nymph dappled with sea foam. He looked at her enraptured. She was his wife, his love, his dream turned real, yet too bewitchingly beautiful for reality.

Suddenly her eyes dilated. Her mouth opened in horror. His eyes followed hers. Behind the window, on the wet ground, a beggar sat, staring God knows where with his blind terrifying eyes. He took her in his arms, and carried her back to the bed, whispering reassuring words into her ear, roseate and translucent like a shell. She fairly trembled with horror: in the blind man she recognized one of the villagers from Pakhom's retinue.

A faint suspicion gripped his heart. "If you open the other shutter," she feverishly whispered, "you will find another beggar."

He swung open the other shutter. There in the corner sat two blind villagers, rigid as gargoyles.

"Dress quickly and quietly," he said. "And down to the market place, where we shall get horses, oh, my own one." He felt as though in a moment he would lose her forever.

Quickly she dressed. Quietly they opened the door. She uttered a shriek of dismay and fell in his arms. At the very threshold, facing them with unseeing murderous pupils, crouched Pakhom. A triumphant smile twisted his walrus mustache.

"Good morning, my lady," he said, jumping to his feet. "How was the . . ." He added six or seven foul words.

"Let us pass," Vladi ordered him, holding his knife in readiness, and figuring quickly where to stab the chieftain.

"Su-u-u-ure," the blind man drawled. "You are going to pass straight to jail, and the Cheka will take good care of your corpses, you dung."

Vladi moved toward the door, dragging Ariadne with him. She was almost unconscious.

"Have you another bottle of that famous vintage you slipped me?" the *starshina* went on. "Blind I am, blind, on account of you, dirty, detestable harlot . . . Brethren, brethren!" he shouted.

The three beggars quickly rose and stumbled against the wall, and bumped their heads against the shutter, and cursed wildly.

"You better lay off that hag," Pakhom warned him. "We'll let you go. All we want is to get hold of this witch, take her with us to the village, and burn her. That's all, so help us God . . ."

Ariadne sobbed hysterically.

"Aha, harlot," Pakhom roared. "You don't like it? Give us back our eyes, give us our sight. I shall pick your eyes and stick them into my sockets, and maybe I'll see yet, maybe we'll see yet. . . ."

"Atma!" he shouted. "Atma!"

Pakhom whistled and burst out laughing. "Magician? Black and white magic you want? Look around and you'll see your sorcerer somewhere."

He gazed into the yard. There he lay, twisted, still alive, groaning, in a puddle of purple blood, his friend Atma, the priest of Orca.

He seized the razor and made a dash for the blind man. Pakhom screamed. Soon, all the four blind beggars were wrestling with him. So enraged was he, that he would have probably slashed them all to pieces. But the sight of one of them, pale, eyeless, sitting on the floor, and convulsively, in agony, searching for a severed finger, filled him with such violent revulsion that he nearly fainted, and dropped the razor. Like a flock of bats they swooped down on him.

Still he would have fought to the very end. But there, in the dark hallway he saw two faces. The two men. Pakhom recognized their footfalls and roared with delight. "Did you get him? Did you get the bastard?"

The two men marched in pompously. Behind them, bleeding and haggard, trudged the old man of the Tsarevich's retinue, and further behind, the Tsarevich himself, his shirt torn to shreds. Ariadne screamed.

"There you are," Pakhom cried out. "You need no

better proof. This witch is behind their scheme to put him back on the throne."

"That's a monstrous lie," Vladi shouted, trembling, alive to the danger of being implicated in the plot. He turned to the tall man with equine teeth, the one who had so lustfully caressed Lidda's hips and thighs.

"We shall administer nothing but justice," the commissar said with a smile.

"Justice, justice," Pakhom muttered. "Give that hag to us. She belongs to us."

She lay unconscious on the bed. The commissar bent over her. Vladi lunged forward, and their eyes met.

"I guess you'll have to forget her for a while," the man said, while his hand caressed her tresses. "You're going to be in different cells."

"In the name of the Republic I arrest you," the other official intervened with a sour grin. He was both jealous of the equine-faced man, and disapproving of his tactics. "Dyakonov, finish it."

"We'll stay in town," Pakhom fussily declared, shuffling childishly here and there. "Pyatakov, Koryto, Salykh, follow me . . . Hold on . . ."

They marched out in Indian file, the very embodiment of an ancient Japanese print. Dyakonov lifted her, and carried her to the door.

"She doesn't weigh much," he remarked, breathing heavily. "Still," he added with a wry smile, "it would not do to carry her thus. Say Lopukhov, take these convicts down to my office, and then send Zotov here with my carriage."

The other, distrusting him, determined not to leave him alone with the beautiful woman, protested. "She is coming to," he said through his teeth. "Let us leave all together."

"Come on, come on," Pakhom's voice was heard outside, and the blind tribe rang out like a second rate chorus in a provincial opera:

"We go, we go. . . ."

They trudged into the street. Grey men and grey women met them and turned aside, afraid to be implicated by a furtive, casual, fatally misinterpreted glance.

"Tuck—tuck—tuck," the blind men's sticks battered the sidewalk, like a weird Madagascar band.

"Turn your face to me," he whispered, "my beloved, my never-to-be-forgotten angelic vision that came to me atop the Aurora Borealis, and beckoned to me like a siren, and bade me follow beyond the icy waves of the wild Northern Sea to plunge into eternal night in quest of you,—Ariadne, found and lost! . . ."

The gate opened. The gate closed. They were in the yard. They were separated. For the last time the pale, dazed face of Ariadne fluttered before his dimmed eyes.

And the dark cell received the Tsarevich and him.
There were three of them—with the violin.

Several days passed. They were down in a dungeon beneath a basement. Through the grated oblong aperture dim shifts of light cast pallid shadows on their grimy faces. They could see and hear the clumsy heavy boots of the guard. It was the same boot every morning.

Most of their time was spent in chasing away the rats. To warm his chilled fingers he played, and the guard paced stealthily, balancing his body on tiptoes, in love with the divine sounds, even as the rats and mice and the one harmless snake that had crept forth, and the centipedes, and the entranced spiders that dangled from the wall.

On the third afternoon the guard permitted him out for a walk in the yard; this in exchange for a rendition of I'll Hire a Troika For My Last Five-spot. Alone in the big yard, he clung to the niches and crevices, peeping here and there, searching the very air for Ariadne. The cool afternoon made him tipsy with the desire for freedom. He surveyed the tomb-like structure, listening with a vague apprehension to the rasping swish of brooms outside. Erstwhile notables, in order to set an awe-inspiring example for the rest of the "criminal bourgeoisie," were forced to spend three hours a day sweeping the sidewalks in front of the prison. Now and then this or that hostage, accused of lack of zeal in his sweeping service, was incarcerated and executed.

The yard was apparently dead. Only once a few men

and women were seen trudging along the wall. But their steps were muffled by the gravel. Except for the broom music, not a sound came from the neighbouring streets.

He returned to the cell, disheartened. The guard, leisurely rolling a cigarette, told him confidentially that five prisoners had been *spent* that very afternoon, among them one woman, very young and pretty.

The Tsarevich embraced him and spoke with gripping sadness. "I have a strange foreboding that something is going to happen to-night."

He solaced him, and entertained him with the story of his adventures in New York and Moscow, of Atma, of the negro and the village. In turn, the boy told him about the life at the Court. He knew everyone, and he spoke with a strange quiver of the one he had loved most—of his mother, the dead Tsarina. His big eyes, moist and agitated, shone with animal intuition. His girlish hands rested in Vladi's as though seeking comfort. He was a beautiful maniac—the loveliest, the most heartrendingly noble type of insanity that ever trod on the face of the earth. And yet, it was surprising how well he remembered every detail of Court receptions, names, patronymics, festivals and places. He never made a mistake, never forgot what he had previously said. He even vaguely intimated that unless he was greatly mistaken the world would soon hear about his sister Tatyana, also believed to have been executed at Ekaterinburg.

"Like me, she feigned death," he whispered, and his hand trembled. "God knows whether she was successful."

"Tell me . . . are you really . . . the son of the . . . Tsar?" He was ashamed to put the question so bluntly, for he loved the boy with all the power of his languishing heart. The boy rose indignantly.

"Leave me alone," he said. Vladi laughed. How could he possibly leave the boy alone in the cell?

"Forgive me, oh, forgive me . . ."

"Never," the boy said firmly. "Leave me alone."

Heavy footsteps thudded nearer and nearer.

"Forgive me, forgive me," he cried piteously. Was he soon to be *spent?* Would he be put out like a candle?

"Never," the boy repeated. "You have doubted the word of a king."

The door opened.

"Stand up!"

"Follow us!"

Four soldiers with sabres unsheathed encircled them. They followed the dancing light of the lamp. Stumbling, they crept through the dank corridors. All the horrors of the Pit and the Pendulum awaited them in that Labyrinth. He hobbled hurriedly after the soldiers.

"Halt!"

The iron door slowly opened, and they found themselves before the two men. Without further ado

Dyakonov asked him how long he had known the so-called Tsarevich, who in reality was the son of a petty army officer in the former tsarist army, and whose real name was Alexey Nikandrov.

He answered these questions, seemingly to their satisfaction. The two men were decidedly not on best of terms, for no sooner had Dyakonov begun to question him concerning Lidda than the other was up in the air. Unmindful of their quibbling, Vladi spoke with bitterness about the woman who had never really been his, and who only mocked him and stalled off their marriage until he was insane with passion. Every night she promised to be his, and yet somehow that jade managed to elude his arms. It was in prison that for the first time he slept soundly, in spite of rats and snakes.

Dyakonov burst into a paroxysm of laughter.

"She played the same trick on comrade Lopukhov," he said between fits of laughter. "You are not the only one."

"It remains to be seen whether you are going to be more successful to-night," the other dryly retorted. He was obviously vexed.

"To-night," he said. So she was alive!

"Never mind," Dyakonov remarked arrogantly. "To-night I shall avenge both of you."

"Perhaps," he mumbled with a low obeisance, "perhaps—if you let me play—for you—the two of you.

. . . She might be more amenable to love. . . ."

"You think so?" Dyakonov inquired, arching his dense brows. "All right, I'll tell the guard. Not a bad idea."

"If you can charm her with your violin, as you claim, like Plutus, then why didn't you use your tricks on her?" Lopukhov asked morosely.

"I did. And it worked, while I played. As soon as I finished playing and tried to make love to her she was cool as a cucumber. What a witch!"

"Let's finish our work," Lopukhov suggested. In their growing hostility there was a faint promise of salvation.

"Bother," Dyakonov dropped with contempt. "Give the boy the third degree, and take this man back to his cell. And let him come at ten o'clock with his violin."

And so they were separated for ever, the lovely Tsarevich and Vladi. Nor did he ever see him again. He could not forget him, as he could not forget the negro, and the bear, and the notary, and thousands of other fugitive faces and figures, except his own. Was he torn to pieces, quartered, broken on the wheel? Was he drowned in the lethal chambers of the Cheka? Or was he merely *spent*, and cast into the common grave in the backyard? No longer dreamy was his lovely face, and the gleam of his moist eyes no longer rested on attentive faces. The scrap heap of Ekaterinburg was now complete.

WHEN he returned to the cell, he found a basket on his cot. The guard told him that an old woman had left the basket with provisions for him on condition that he share the drinks with him. There was a big loaf of dark rye bread, two cakes, a bottle of vodka and a pamphlet on the Life of Lenin. He was lost in surmises. Who could have thought of him? Lidda surely would not thus betray their intimacy, and Atma was dead.

He poured half of the vodka in the guard's canteen, and their friendship was now eternal. The guard promised to drink only *that* much a day, but an hour later his container was empty, and he sadly peeped through the grate and eyed the intact supply of liquor.

Indifferent to the food, he took a swig of the quickening liquor. The guard, watching him, moaned. He let him have another drink and cut the bread to offer him half a loaf. As he did so, he checked with difficulty an outcry of surprise; embedded in the thick dough lay a thin dagger of the finest steel. The point had been carefully wrapped in several layers of cotton, and he did not hasten to unwrap these, for right near the blade he found a scrap of paper bearing this inscription: *very poison.* It was Atma's style. In fact, the pamphlet contained two words underlines, as if casually—one on page 7 and the other on page 8—*I,* and *Alive.* At the end of the tract there was the reassuring word: Atma.

So he was alive, his faithful friend, the sorcerer and

priest of Orca! The whole basket became vested with new mysteries. He scrutinized every crumb, he examined and unpasted every label. There, on the obverse side of the bottle-label he found Atma's own statement: "Now I live Wet Street number 11."

He wrapped the stiletto and hid it under the violin in the box. Dream or no dream, reality or relativity, whatever life was, the dagger was destined to penetrate a human breast and pave the way to freedom.

Night came. The rats bestirred themselves. Now there was no one to keep them away, and they grew bolder. He threw crumbs of bread in all directions, and soon the cell resounded with angry gnarling and hissing. Ragingly they fought over particularly appetizing bits. He squatted on his cot, watching the wicked flash of their eyes.

"Come out," he suddenly heard the guard's voice.

He hugged his violin and followed the guard. Faint groans reached them on both sides of the dark alley. Two men and a woman were to be executed in the early hours of the morning (the guard had told him so). There were too many British spies around, and the Red Guards were in a desperate state.

The dungeons were plunged into darkness. Only in Dyakonov's room could one sense rather than see a dim light through the thick curtain. He knocked at the door—and entered.

On the sofa near the writing desk, lay Ariadne, nude as a Giorgione Venus. Her face was beautiful in its pallor. He feared to look at her too intently, for he felt the steel, haunting glance of the commissar. They remained silent and motionless for a moment.

"Well, how do you like your wife?" Dyakonov asked.

"Not so . . . very . . much," he stuttered, spitting with disgust. "Don't flatter yourself, comrade commissar. This damn harlot will strip for any high bidder."

"I can see you're still a bit jealous," Dyakonov remarked, not displeased. "She'll like me all right. She'll have to."

"She'll have to!" he exclaimed with delight. "At last we'll have the best of her. I'd love to see the jade forced into submission, the harlot! Lord, how she made me suffer!"

Dyakonov laughed with genuine merriment. The situation seemed to amuse him vastly. A resentful husband chortling over the downfall of his own wife was too much for him, and he sneezed, and reached for his red kerchief to wipe his nose, and for a second or two Vladi gazed at Ariadne, breathing heavily, as if he were to succumb to the magnetic force of her nudity. But the man was watching them—the suspicious Asiatic— and for a moment he though that his eyes betrayed him, and the commissar was ready to press the button, or else to reach for his Circassian dagger dangling down his beautiful Caucasian cassock adorned with silver cartridges.

"How was she to-night?" Vladi whispered in the manner of an intimate conspirator. "Any more tractable?"

"Just a little bit," Dyakonov replied. "But look at her. Isn't she beautiful? Look at her breasts, they're such lovely hillocks! And her belly . . . And . . ."

"Let me play," he interrupted him. "She has always had a strange penchant for music . . . Few people, in fact, can resist good music."

Dyakonov sat near her. She did not budge. He took her palm in his and stroked her breasts.

"Music, huh?" Vladi cried. "Shall I play?"

"Be careful," Ariadne was saying. "I told you how far you can go."

"Who is giving orders in this place?" Dyakonov snapped angrily. "You're starting the damn thing all over again."

"You can't have me without my consent," she continued. "I may love you to-morrow, what do you know? Isn't love like a caprice? Be good and you won't regret it."

He stared at her with bloodshot eyes. "You're a witch. How beautiful you are! . . . That throat, those eyes. . . ."

"Can't you act like a gentleman?" she asked ingratiatingly, stroking his mane. "And . . . let . . . let . .

. let him play . . . I do love his music, even if I hate him and his impotent drivelling."

Dyakonov doubled up with laughter.

He opened the violin case. The dagger lay on the red plush like a baby lizard basking in the sun. Tears came into his eyes. He thought he had heard a faint note of animosity in her disparaging remark about him. Did she really hate him? He played Weniawski's *Legend*, then Tschaikovski's *Canzonetta*, and other melodious and stirring things he knew she liked.

"God, but you play beautifully," Dyakonov said wiping his forehead. Like all lascivious men, he was very sentimental. He made a move to embrace Ariadne. She slipped out of his arms, and jumped into the corner, ready to use her fingernails.

"Don't be stupid!" Vladi exclaimed. "Sooner or later you'll have to belong to him. Why not now?"

"Yes, why not now?" Dyakonov chimed in, his masculine vanity deeply offended.

"Or do you treat all men the way you treat me?" he inquired venomously. "Good Lord, if I were he, I'd murder you, I'd flay you, mangy harlot! . . ."

Still she did not look at him. Was she aware of the comedy he was enacting? Did she read his thoughts? She stood in the corner, bent, aquiver, determined.

"Come on, embrace him," he said angrily. "I don't care, you'll never be mine again. . . . Embrace him, show him your heart isn't of stone. Wasn't he good to us? He could have killed us without trial. Instead, he spared our lives. Embrace him. And stroke his arms, and press him tightly to your thighs, tightly, tightly, the way you once pressed mine."

A gleam of light flashed in her eyes. She understood.

"All right," she said gingerly, as if giving in. "But don't be rough." And while she snuggled on the sofa and whispered words of love, he played *Black Eyes, Sad Eyes*.

"You're a magician," Dyakonov said, when he stopped to tune up the violin. "I'll remember it, believe me."

He fiercely turned the peg. A string *had to* burst. He *had to* go to the box.

"Even as I told you," he modestly replied. "But don't you think you have an unjust advantage over comrade Lopukhov?"

Dyakonov's lusty laughter was cut short by the wailing sound of a broken string.

"Oh, it'll be fixed in a second," he quickly reassured him. "I have several strings in the case." And he rushed to the case.

Quickly he returned and sat on the chair near the sofa to adjust a new string. Ariadne held Dyakonov's arms as if to ward off his persistent fumbling. As he glanced at her, she strengthened her grip.

"See this string?" Vladi asked mockingly. "It's no good. It's false. And here is a dagger dipped in the most deathly poison known to man. One prick and life is gone."

"What are you talking there?" Dyakonov mumbled amazedly, between kisses. "Play!"

"One prick and death!" he hissed suddenly, bending over him. "Don't rise, do you hear me? One move and you are dead!"

Yet he did make a move to get his two revolvers. They were gone. Ariadne had them. Like a snake she slipped from the sofa.

"You heard what this man said," she warned him. "We shan't shoot you, that'd make too much noise. But just say another word, and you'll die noiselessly and thoroughly."

"Go and dress quickly," Vladi ordered her, "and keep the revolvers right near you. I'll take care of him."

The last adventure was over. Had anything interfered then between Ariadne and himself, he would have driven the dagger into his own heart. He was tired.

"About face," he commanded. "Stand up and walk to the middle of the room and then stand still."

Like an automaton Dyakonov carried out the orders. He was very pale. Ariadne dressed. The revolvers in her hands, she stood nearby.

"Here is the telephone," he said. "Just repeat what I say."

"You'll regret it," Dyakonov murmured. "You'll pay with your lives for it."

"Come on, quit your nonsense," he sternly said. "You better watch out for your own . . . Now, call up the commissar of the building and order him to have two horses ready for this woman and myself . . . Now, talk!"

Dyakonov stared at them with intense hatred. Nothing can equal the rage of a male separated from his female just when he thinks he had passed through all stages of preliminary courtship and is ready for the final conquest. Breathing heavily, he leaned forward, in a vain attempt to seize the stiletto. The needlepoint of the dagger almost grazed his face. He shrank back and falteringly repeated the order.

"That's better," Vladi commanded him. "Now tell him not to wake you up until ten o'clock in the morning, for you're very very busy and going to work late to-night. That'll be all."

He repeated the order in a dull military manner.

"Now write out a pass for both of us," Vladi orderd. He felt a strange weakness benumb his gestures. His temples were burning. Would he fail again, on the eve of complete freedom? Something stronger than his will carried him on.

He carefully reread the pass and examined the seal.

"Hurry, my beloved," Ariadne suddenly exclaimed, and he saw fear, and love, and passion in her large eyes.

"One moment," he interrupted her. "Let me have all the keys of the building and the gate . . . And not a word, *comprenez?*"

He found a big rope in the drawer (how many girlish throats had it strangled?) and fighting a weird nauseating revulsion that was rising in his heart, he tied and gagged the man so that he could hardly breathe, and shoved him under the table.

It was past midnight. The yard was dark grey, the walls a dab of white in the thick night. All was quiet. Ariadne held on to his arm and suddenly, unable to check all the pent up emotions that tore him asunder, he drew her near to him and fiercely pressed his lips upon her mouth, and kissed her frantically, whispering words that were sheer madness. Her body hung limply in his arms. "Oh . . . let's go," she managed to whisper. Gladly would he have died there, in the somber yard of the Inquisitors. He did not want to flee into the night with her. Some strange force had projected him onto a diminutive puppet stage, and his feet were strangely recalcitrant.

"Let . . . us . . . go," she begged. He gave her the violin, and bade her wait. He had decided to free half a dozen prisoners, to keep the authorities busy in the morning. It seemed desirable to dissipate the energy of the officials, if they were to be saved. But it was too dark, and he could not even find the proper keys. And then, the first prisoner, upon hearing his voice thought him one of the executioners and raised such a heartrending howl, that he had to desist. Luckily, in that dungeon a human howl meant nothing. He returned to Ariadne.

Hugging the ghostly wall, she trembled with agitation.

"Away, away from here," she sobbed in his ear. They crept to the gate. The commissar, a huge, square-faced peasant, examined their papers, and opened the rusty iron gate.

They dashed along the deserted streets. When they neared Wet Street he whistled. Lidda stopped.

He slid to the small house, his finger on the trigger, and whistled drawingly, imitating the Cheremiss' signal. The moon appeared from behind the rim of the cloud. He whistled again.

"Hear?" Ariadne whispered.

Indeed, the muffled sound of Atma's answer reached his ear. Soon his shadow emerged from behind the gate. He jumped over the fence, and rushed to them, shaking their hands, nodding his head excitedly. It was the first time that they saw him so stirred.

"I'll get a horse, don't worry," he said. "You go straight to Arkhangel, I join you in an hour on the road. Yes? Only give me the dagger, huh?"

He gave him the blade, and soon they were again dashing along the moonlit road towards Arkhangel. Now and then he looked behind. What if *he* tore off his gag, and roared for help, what if they were galloping behind them?

"Ariadne," he shouted, "I am trembling with cold."

It was a natural reaction to all he had gone through in the last days. He pictured Lopukhov peeping in through the keyhole to see whether his rival had been bested. Silence. . . . And the amorous fights? And the erotic combats accompanied by bacchic clamoring? Silence. He is aroused . . .

"Ariadne," he shouted, "I can hear them following us, a hundred Red Guards, a regiment, a whole division!"

"I am with you," she whispered. He could not hear her. He guessed the words. The moon disappeared, and a green veil shrouded her face. Why was she hiding?

They galloped and galloped. Around them lay marshy wasteland. Here and there an islet of bushes rose like a sinister spectre and waved at them its fanlike crown. Soon dawn greeted them with a grey slit of a smile at the horizon. They were alone. He was feverish. His head burned.

"Ariadne!" he cried. "How far are we from New York?"

"Stop," her voice came through the fog. "What do you say?"

They stopped. He staggered in the saddle. "Where's your father now?" he asked. "God, I've got so many symphonies to write yet!"

Lidda sobbed. It was Lidda, beyond any doubt, not

Ariadne. How could he have mistaken her for Ariadne? "Wake up! Wake up!" she cried.

But he was awake. For a moment he regained consciousness. "How my tongue burns!" he moaned. "I'm broken in all my limbs. Lidda, Ariadne! I am dying."

She led his horse to the forest.

"Ah," he roared. "You want to kill me, witch! Wait till I get hold of you, assassin!"

He kicked her with his boot. She clutched at him, galloping at a steady pace to the forest. As they entered it, he lost all consciousness of what was going on. He saw her face as pale as a new moon. How he hated her! He sought to thrust his revolver at her beastly breast, but his limbs were leaden. She took away his weapon. He sobbed hopelessly. He knew she was going to murder him in that forest where no human foot had ever trod.

"Don't kill!" he begged. He heard the hoofs of the squad on the road. The witch rose, to steer them off the path, into the thicket, and to deliver him to them. Oh, why had he returned the blade to Atma? He could have stabbed her right there, and saved himself. No doubt, both had plotted his death.

With the last effort of his sagging muscles, he lunged forward clutching for her throat. But his fingers were numb. Someone dragged him farther into the thicket. A girlish voice rang in his ears. They were nearing Arkhangel. A sweet lovely face bent over him and suddenly everything disappeared in the melting snow that swept over him like a torrent. Amidst the rising guffaws of the triumphant waves he saw her, Ariadne. Rocked to deadly slumber by dull despair, he closed his eyes and rolled down the gigantic cataract into a watery ravine. And the dream began.

Undoubtedly what subsequently transpired could not have been reality. The visions were grotesque and incoherent and all sequence was tangled. It was as if an impish child had played a trick on the dull teacher and—merely to disrupt the deadening parade of cause and effect—blurted out, spitefully: "To-morrow, I have seen him. And yesterday she shall die!" And yet the reality of that dream was at least as palpable as the dreaminess of all our realities.

But much as his sagging mind revelled in the loosely connected dreamy episodes, it was wracked beyond endurance by the sudden appearance and final and irreparable loss of Ariadne, the light of his life. It was all a dream, of course, a horrid dream; and its burden weighed upon his soul already overwhelmed with burdens of former realities. He awoke and collapsed, and awoke again in a bleak forest. Someone dragged him somewhere. Hope was gone. Strange faces leaned over him. He was shouting with terror when his eyes caught a glimpse of the azure sky overhead, which filled his soul with boundless serenity. Quite pronounced was the consciousness that all had been a dream, and the torrential sweep of melting snow might also have been a dream. Convulsively he jumped to his feet. The sun was high and baked his shaved head. His nude shoulders began to burn.

Through intruding lianas that crept everywhere with

a joyous exuberance, he walked, at once aware that the thicket was alive. Seemingly dead in the day, the forest pulsated life at night. Repellent monkeys were laughing high in the branches and threw hard shells at him. As he proceeded, the darkness softened into an even grey all-pervading light. He noticed the gorgeous colors of the red-blue, flaming birds. Yellow, red, green parrots stared at him with an idiotic fixedness.

The colorfulness of that forest was weirdly dimmed by a pleasant twilight. Not a harsh sound, not a loud color; all was subdued by an invisible force that seemed to move about that grotesque domain. Over all there swam a soft, unforgettable cacophony of irreconcilable chords. So beautifully unreal was it all, that for a moment he thought he witnessed a scene from "Life is a Dream," as he had once imagined it while reading.

And yet he was quite certain that it was not a dream. His benumbed legs were taxed to the utmost trying to avoid clods, trunks, and stumps, and to dodge strange reptiles with agilely wagging tongues and wicked bulging eyes.

Just how long he marched thus he could never quite ascertain. Day and night meant nothing in his dream. An everlasting twilight reigned there; morning or noon, the same rippling cacophony, to which his ears and eyes grew accustomed, filled the vaporous air. He lost all hope of reaching Arkhangel, or of ever seeing Ariadne.

Every step entangled him more and more in the dense brushwood of that man-trap. The first few days (?) he cried with helplessness . . . Instead of nearing New York, he thought, every step he took drove him into the very heart of some unknown South American region. Even the soil there possessed an uncanny witchcraft, for his tears, falling on the mossy ground, stirred thin pillars of sulphurous fumes.

Soon he approached a little grove on the shore of a crystalline lake. Graceful trees reached high into the sky, now visible through the enchanted thinning forest. Emerging from the last row of the arboreal rampart, he sighed with relief. It was as though he had become a child again. The moppy tops of the trees greeted him with a gentle murmur. Under the sharply cut edge of the opposite shore he could see slender trees reflected in the mirrory surface of the lake. He was so happy to be out of the forest, that he began to leap with exultation. Gentle silver-breasted pigeons gathered round him, confidently settling on his shoulders. He kissed their tender heads. Beautiful children! This was the end of his gruesome journey. Could there be any doubt that the beautiful lake was at the gate of some lovely village or town?

Indeed, a group of people was slowly moving toward him, apparently unaware of his presence. Already he could discern the tangled locks of the bearded man's head. Near him an elderly matron was proceeding in a rather pompous fashion. Their two children were gayly leaping about them.

"What a blissful encounter!" he exclaimed. Quickly the family surrounded him and listened with undisguised curiosity to his effusions. The bearded man chuckled, but seemed to resent the children's merriment, for he shoved them aside, and they lost much of their spontaneous joyfulness . . . He suddenly noticed that the lower part of his body virtually sunken in tall grass was covered with thick wool: his feet were equine. He surmised then that he had met a centaur family.

The old man was very sedate, and quite amusing in his solemn superiority. So was his spouse. But the children were of exquisite beauty. The boy like a young colt frolicked and gambolled around Vladi, shoving his lovely graceful hoofs into his pockets, or flattening his funny little nose against his abdomen. He wanted to take him in his arms, but like a timorous pup he darted away. Then, from behind a tall pine, the young centaur hailed him and made such grimaces that he roared with laughter.

"Where did you hitch up with this funny creature?" the old centaur asked, scratching his wiry locks.

"I picked him up in the forest," he suddenly heard Atma's apologetic voice.

"The nerve of the fakir!" he wanted to shout, but the cry died on his lips as he noticed the strange metamorphosis Atma had undergone: he was now fourlegged, woolly hair covering his breast and legs. Now he shook his curly head and winked.

"Illusions!" he thought he heard him whisper.

Once more he was alone, in the power of the bloodthirsty centaur tribe. So after all, the Cheremiss magician was nothing but a centaur in disguise roaming over open roads like a doomed soul, and seducing weary travellers into swamps!

The soil was crumbling under his feet. His heart slowly sank under the threatening looks of those beasts. Fortunately, the old centaur seemed to be of a somewhat benevolent disposition.

"Say, what did they do to the other half of his body?" he asked disparagingly.

"Your females are no better, two-legged as they are," Vladi snapped back at him.

Nevertheless the centaur had the last word.

"They are women," he said, "and not much can be expected from them either in the topmost or nethermost parts of their body." Which settled the argument.

It is impossible to say how the centaur family would have disposed of his wretched days. But the silvery voice of the girl put an end to the painful uncertainty of the situation.

"Give me that funny thing," she said. "I want a toy."

And thus he was bestowed upon the exquisite dryad.

"We'll always have enough time to kick him to death," the patriarch said, "in case baby gets tired of him. His father had driven mine into the feedless forests, away from the fragrant groves that belonged to our tribe."

"Let me go, I beseech you," he cried, realizing that his prison would last a lifetime. "I must see a girl named Ariadne! Without me she'll pine away with anxiety."

The brute kicked him in the shins with such force that he fell on his back. He realized that all human feelings were strange to their souls, and began to sob.

"Look, look," the centaur's daughter exclaimed, "look at the round pearls that drop from his eyes."

And she went about collecting his tears in her palm, smelling them, and licking them with her sharp tongue. She was aflame with curiosity. She pressed her nude body to his, seemingly to investigate the origin and nature of tears, unknown to their half-animal nature. It was then he noticed how beautiful she was. The most superb Galatea in marble could not compare with the severe harmony of her lines. Not a dot on her smooth body to mar the velvety surface. She was fragrant with wild flowers; her breath was hot and exciting. She must have noticed how pale he grew when she pressed her body to his, for she laughed tauntingly. The silvery tinkle of her mocking voice was caught up by the breeze.

"Carry me," she commanded, and in a moment her fiery body bestrode his shoulders. She twisted her long legs around his body and urged him on with an ecstatic pressure of her thighs. Blood rushed to his head. The warmth of her imprisoning thighs was truly indescribable. He wanted to dash onward, on wings of a surging breeze, but his knees bent under him, and they fell.

But she did not loosen her grip. Amidst loud outbursts of joy, they rolled in the luscious grass, enlaced like ivy. Her madness made his heart palpitate with an ominous vehemence. He vaguely felt that her innocent fingers were searching his pockets. Several times he had the best of her, feverishly holding her hands and preventing her from sticking them into his trousers, the sole remainder of his clothing. At last, she snatched off his garment. Upon seeing him naked, she began to struggle with him in a fit of sudden ecstasy. He fell into a state of utter helplessness. She was Fate.

Suddenly she whispered: "My name, too, is Ariadne. From me they all get their loveliness."

Incredible bliss poured through his veins. Amid the rude laughter of the centaurs they forgot themselves and floated in vapors of an unforgettable dream.

And thus he became a member of the centaur family. His marriage to Ariadne was celebrated by a savage dance on the huge meadow adjoining the grove. The little centaur, who had a ridiculous habit of thrusting his oblong face into everybody's armpit like a blind puppy, jumped over the fire with a wild Ya-ho, Ya-ho!

How he loved his little brother-in-law, in spite of all his annoying pranks! He often embraced him, now that the boy no longer was afraid of him. The young centaur quickly fell asleep in his arms, mumbling fragments of the day's impressions, reminiscences of a dialogue with a thrush, or angry remarks to a recalcitrant turtle that had told him to leave her alone and stop turning her on her back. After the flying embers had hissed their last breath, and the centaur had imbibed so abundantly that he, literally, began to stumble on all fours, Ariadne, excited by the bacchic saltations dragged him to the cool cavern, which his father-in-law had given him as a nuptial gift.

Soft-limbed was Ariadne, resilient of breast. She talked continuously, but her topics bore no relation to her or him. Like a child, she prattled of flowers and relatives, of an invitation transmitted to her by the wind to be present at the wedding of a doe, a distant relative of hers; of the death of an aged turtle, that once upon a time used to be her nurse; of a visit to Bacchus, who lived in a neighboring grotto. What dream she made him dream! How he dreaded the moment of awakening! The dreamy undulations of her voice were by no means reassuring. They were so entrancingly melodious that they could form part only of a dream. He felt her arms, he slipped his hands lower, lower, to the torrid witchery of her thighs—and shouted with ecstasy. A dream or not a dream? But the dream of yesterday is like the reality of yesterday, and the realities of yore are like the dreams of yore. He squirmed in agony. He wanted to strangle her. If she no longer existed, would it not prove that she had existed before?

But she raised her long finger to her roguish mouth . . . Not now . . . Wait . . .

She dragged him to the grotto.

On their way back to the cavern, as he bent down to pick up a frog, the old centaur, liquor-soaked and tottering, kicked him so violently that he roared with rage. Was he becoming centaurish himself? The old brute hiccoughed pitifully, a helpless half-man at a crossroads. His wife was sitting near him, like an old squaw at the corpse of her husband. She was apparently gratified at the plight of her husband, her perennial tormentor. He cried, and a strange tearless lament it was. Vladi embraced him and wiped his sweat with a big leaf.

Between hiccoughs the tipsy centaur complained of the dire lot of the vanishing centaur tribe. Only a few dozen of them had survived to roam in the constantly narrowing groves whither man's greed had driven them with ax and sawmill. Only a few years earlier, he had dined with Bacchus' children, and Pan himself had played at his wedding. Now Pan was hiding, and only the doleful sough of his fifes rolled over the hilltops. Some day even these signs of his waning existence would disappear.

While he thus lamented, Vladi watched his erstwhile companion, now a newly born member of the anthropoid tribe. The hypocrite pretended to slumber. An apologetic smile hovered over his lips. How skilfully, how imperceptibly that magician abducted men and cast them into the net of illusions!

Strangely enough, he could not be angry at him too long. That grove was his home, and Ariadne was his mistress and wife. He felt as though he had never had parents. He thought of his past as of a flickering film seen somewhere, now of little consequence, not worthy of a lengthy remembrance. The idyllic slumber of his little brother-in-law filled him with more tenderness than all the witchcraft of his native Moscow river and its dreamy flow. He bent over him, and kissed his delightfully pursed lips.

The gentle melody of a flute wailed over the motionless tree-tops. Evening came. The rubescent horizon looked at them, and the silvery surface of the lake, as white as a mirror, sent cool greetings to the evening star. In the grove a chorus of night birds answered its own echo. Suddenly and without much tuning the frogs gingerly blew into their tremulous bassoons. Ariadne, vainly seeking caresses, was strangely silent on his knees. The

magician, with whom he was not on speaking terms,
dozed near the old centaur.

Thus they sat until dawn.

A UTUMNAL splendor of a waning September. . . .
He felt it in the silent struggle of silver and
gold foliage. The silvery lining of leaves was turning
brown and yellow, like lard on a frying pan. A crystal
lake mirrored numberless hues among shrubs and trees
leaning over the bank with a sad curiosity, intent on
witnessing their own death and the dissolution of their
color-tissue. It was the beauty of the Golden Gate Park
in Autumn, when the rising gentle veil of pale-blue mist
is dissipated into an insistent softness, turns blue into
azure, and pours a milky shade over the dark-green.
There was wine in the air.

The old centaur rose in the morning, caustic and
supercilious as though nothing had happened. Then he
took the boy on a foray to the grove.

Ariadne slipped off his knees and plucked jagged
grassblades out of the steamy earth and sent them high
in the air with a whiff of her breath. Like a demigod he
looked at her, immortal in his bliss. His heart was like
a placid mountain lake. Not a breeze stirred it. When
he glanced beneath its pewter surface he saw his serene
face blazing with strength and pride, the lordly sense
of power that only possession of beauty can arouse.
Ariadne had instilled that new feeling of sovereignty
into his soul.

Her tenderness was beyond description. He loved
her so frantically that he cursed at his human form that

seemed in a way to have prejudiced her against him. For as much as she loved him, she was grieved over his lack of physical perfection. In her eyes he had only half a body, and no amount of persuasion on his part could induce her to revise her standards in judging true symmetry.

The desire to come up to that standard was so overwhelming in him that, much to his surprise, the lower part of his body became gradually furred with a whimsical growth of shaggy hair. He was both delighted and stupefied. Was Atma right, and did will-power create illusions? Ariadne was exultant and overwhelmed him with her passionate caresses. At last he had become one of her own!

As days passed, he grew to love that dream-like girl more and more. Her long body was ever in his arms or on his shoulders. He darted madly past gloriously brown autumnal bushes. She spurred him on with her glowing legs. "Ya-ho! Ya-ho!" she shouted, and they charged through the air and fell on the all-embracing ground and lost themselves in beatific passion.

The crickets rasped their trills and the bumblebee hummed uninterruptedly. He lifted his hand and his fingers grew longer, long like hollow reeds. He touched the grass and each blade responded with a clear and joyful sound. He touched the twigs and from each a sustained tone issued. The world was full of hidden harmony, and it yielded its treasure to every touch of his burning fingers. He lifted his palms and lowered them, and the lake and the dales and the hillocks opened their invisible crevices and froze in a miraculous sweet chord. She gazed at him in silent wonderment.

"You come from a strange race," she said. "But I adore you, even if you are not yet fully ours. Long ago I heard that your kind is fickle and forgets everything after a limited span of years."

"That's why they are so strong," he answered. "They don't let the burden of past affections weigh down upon them. Of the past they keep only such remembrances as will tend to harden them and sharpen their teeth for battles. They remember stupid generals and saintly hypocrites who preached war, but they will eradicate memories of past love, of Eloise and Abelard or Casanova, from the memory of young generations. For love tends to weaken men."

"What is love?" she asked.

"I don't know. Men pretend to know. But they lie. You are love."

She laughed and hid her face in her palms. He disengaged her fingers and drugged his mind with her kisses. His mighty Centaur chest heaved with joy. Nothing marred the peace of their deathless existence. He had reached the pinnacle of life. His beloved never left him. If he could only bid the moment stand! . . . In the morning after a night of endless tales, they played their erotic postludes. The latent music of their voices was relegated to a secondary place by the revelations of her scorching breath; and not even the soothing sting of moments of slumber could untwine their embrace or subdue the intensity of their desires.

In the morning, she was the first to open her almond-shaped eyes. Now and then the impish little centaur peeped into the dark cool grotto, and blew cold water at them through a long hollow reed. They jumped up and ran after him, but it was well-nigh impossible to overtake him. He ran like the wind. His godfather was Pan himself, and as soon as he invoked his help, his feet became winged. From behind a thick bush he mocked them. They dashed after him, but again he soared high into the air, his feet scarcely touching the ground, his arms lifted, plucking leaves and twigs in his flight. Then he dropped somewhere beyond their reach.

Exhausted by this hectic race, they left him alone, and returned languorously to their cavern with the inextinguishable flame of love in their eyes. All the yearnings of his life, sublimated into one torrential desire, burst forth at the very contact of her virgin love. Even her constant prattle was a source of delight to him, for he began to realize that it proceeded from her charming naïveté rather than from a tendency, alas! so common to women. She told him they had been together for fifty days. How did she know? He had no calendar. He did not count the days. Time flowed, an intrinsic part of rivers and clouds. For though the distinction of day and night was recognized in that grove, no one ever seemed to keep track of the days, and there were no names for them.

As for Ariadne, she measured time by the flight of the birds, by the reddening of leaves, by the drooping of tired weeds, by the fits of distemper of her father, who had rheumatism. Her unity with nature was complete and she had no need to count the days, no more than a nightingale needs solfeggio lessons.

So fifty days had passed in the ecstasy of love, in a thousand and one tricks of inventive amorous fancy, in flights of fervid passions. Often it happened that they dreamed the same dreams as if the nocturnal thoughts had passed from his disturbed brain into hers through his endless kisses. This amused her greatly. Once he dreamed of his mother singing the familiar song about the white goat setting out on a journey into unknown lands, to bring fragrant raisins for the devoted Bible-student; all of which happened to be the content of the second couplet of the same cradle song. At another time, both of them dreamt of a male quartette, four negroes, in high hats, devilishly slim, in tight black trousers, swinging their canes and singing *Down in Dixie*. She was puzzled by the strange melodies, even though charmed by the unusual tempo of those strains so different from her conception of music. And he dwelt at length on the wonders of Negro music. He resolved that as soon as they reached the States he would take her to a vaudeville theatre, and show her some real entertainment.

In spite of the piercing cold of the dry, sunlit winter-air, they took long walks to the other side of the lake. He built a small raft, and they paddled across, Ariadne reclining near the very edge of the raft and bathing her palm in the foaming wave. They breached the raft in a mountain-bordered cove. There they were free to gaze into the quiet water, undisturbed by the laments of the old man, or by the pranks of the boy. They were gradually drifting away from their family. Ariadne had completely filled his life, and no other desires ever agitated his heart or brain. He hollowed out a long reed, and blew into it, and produced meditative, plaintive sounds almost as perfectly sustained as the incomparable breath of Pan himself. Ariadne, lying on her breast, her lovely chin in cupped palms, listened to his melodies.

Now and then an equatorial storm disrupted their idyll. The strange storms of that season! . . . There was no rain, nor snow in that region. All Nature ran dry, tortured like a human being, twisted and gagged and denied the power of relieving his torture by sobbing. The sky never wept. But a sudden purple-red tinge spread over the entire landscape, and the bloodshot earth burst out into howlings. At such moments Ariadne, distressed, threw up her arms and flung herself straight into his reassuring embrace. Neither in Europe nor in America, had he ever seen such red storms; and when he was caught in one for the first time, he shook with fear. They ran like trapped animals, looking for shelter. He rushed from tree to tree, with Ariadne on his back. She clung to him like a tired child.

Before the storm, sensing the impending tornado, she had grown restless with vague forebodings, like a lamb uttering plaintive cries. He drew her to him, and it was then they decided to leave that valley of dry red storms forever. He took her on his back, and their devilish race began. In a fit of terror, afraid of the unceasing laughter of the red bushes and howling earth, she sobbed and begged him to speed on. Soon she slid around him, her feet clasped behind his back. Her body tickled his nose, her nails drove into his long curls. All the fragrance of maple leaves, all the dizzying freshness of the lake were in her.

The stars disappeared, the sky grew redder, and suddenly the orange moon appeared in the flame. Exhausted by the maddening flight, he stumbled on a ghostly desiccated trunk and fell. Ariadne uttered a cry of pain as she fell over him and covered his body with the pall of her marvellous hair.

An irrepressible fright seized his soul. The long

drawn howling grew more morbid, carried far away through the furiously swishing bowed tops of the trees.

. . .

He frantically embraced Ariadne, who was wriggling in his arms, moaning words in a strange dialect, almost inarticulate, like the guttural sobs of a tigress. Half dead with terror, he found enough courage to caress her limp body and whisper her beloved name. He wanted to continue the flight, but his body seemed to have grown into the soil. At the same time a feeling of cloyingly sweet forgetfulness fettered his limbs.

Soon the moon disappeared. The howling subsided. Still he did not raise his head. He was certain that there, right near him, someone was standing, big bull-like eyes piercing his spine. A premonition of disaster wrung his heart.

"Ariadne! Ariadne!" he shouted and stretched out his arms to protect her.

But he was alone in the valley, the same valley that he had often visited on his trips around the lake. The dream of Ariadne vanished. Another dream came in its wake. The lake was no more. Aloft he saw the hill from which he had so suddenly slid in his attempt to save Ariadne.

Like a dog he tore the bushes round him, shouting Ariadne! Ariadne! imploring her to cease teasing him, and to show her lovely face.

But the soft melody of the breeze was the only answer. He ran all over the meadow, crying, wringing his fingers, sobbing his woes to the grass, vaguely hoping that she, daughter of the wind, might get the message from the blades with which she had been so friendly.

When he lifted his head he saw Atma sitting near him, watching his mourning in respectful silence. So dazed was his mind that he expressed no amazement at seeing the erstwhile centaur.

"Laws of nature," the other sighed, "are inexorable, when it comes to death. You'd have to part with Ariadne some day, wouldn't you? You can't love eternally, not even in a dream. Suppose she had died?"

"She has not died," he sobbed helplessly. "Oh, my love, my child, my mother and sister, Ariadne! Ariadne! The trunks of trees, the blades of grass, the swaying flower-laden branches, the whole world shaped itself into lovely outlines suggesting various parts of your divine body, now roaming somewhere in eternity. . . ."

"She may be dead or not, but as far as you are concerned she certainly is dead."

"The thought that some day we might see each other."

"Years will pass, and by that time she will be old and wrinkled like her mother, the imperturbable centauress."

"When she is old and ugly, I'll love her as passionately as now." Then he cried out: "Oh, make a miracle, Atma, you who have such power! I'll be your slave, I'll work all my life without any hope of reward, but show her to me, show her form, her fingers vibrant with life."

And he threw himself in the dust, and embraced his feet and kissed his toes. Atma pushed him aside.

He stared at the trees. He believed in miracles. Wasn't his encounter with Ariadne one? The tickling thrust of her brother's long face lingered in his armpit. The resources of nature were tremendous. The trunk of the tree sheltered her, and out of the pale bark the lovely features of his wife would emerge . . . Pan, godfather of the young centaur, the same young imp whose sister was Ariadne, was pouring his melodies over his head. . . . He trembled with despair.

"Illusions," the Cheremiss said quietly. "Illusions of illusions. . . . Fiction and dust. . . . Isn't the dream of yesterday like the reality of centuries ago? And where is Zeena?"

"Zeena from the hill adorned valley,
On the embankment of a raging sea,
Slender thighs and drawn shades,
And the quick fall of rustling bloomers,
Clean little German girl!
And one day she left for Africa,
Never to return again. . . ."

What was he saying? His lips were moving, but he heard no sound. The figure he had evoked emerged on the aërial screen and passed before his eyes.

"Where is she?" Atma asked.

"She is alive, she is," he exclaimed, thrusting his fingers into the air, hoping against hope to put an end to the disruption of his dream.

His arms drooped limply, and he whispered:

"Manushak, the frail Armenian,
From the infernal streets of Stamboul,
In a dingy house of wet shadows . . .
The sounds of viola, and the whirling
Of a young naked body, thrill-thrill –
Ecstasy of triumphant nakedness, octopus
Devouring flame. . . .
One day I disappeared
Never to see her again. . . ."

"Where is she now?" the man asked again.

"I know where she is," he shouted, "and should I desire to see her, I could go back to Constantinople and—and kiss her, the beautiful, the desolate, the unfortunate." He wept.

"But you won't go, you know it. She is dead, dead, dead to you. Her life is wasting away, and after you she has probably had a score of other lovers. Dead, but what of it? Consider her a shadow, a projection. You are no more grieved over the passing of a shadow, when the sun has disappeared."

Unable to check the convulsive flood of reminiscences, he continued:

"In a madly darting train, crammed
With bodies on floor, shelves, roofs, steps.
I in the corner, choking. But you, near me.
So exquisite, young, tender on the
Filth of the train floor. At night you
Were mine. On my knees in the howling
Night of the steppe, the shaking of our bodies,
The rattle of the wheels.

And in the morning, at a God-
Forsaken station you slipped away,
Never to be seen again. . . ."

"Do you remember her face?" the man queried.

"Yes, never-to-be-forgotten. . . ."

"Dead, dead, to you," the man sighed, and shook his head, the hypocrite.

Sobs welled in his heart. There they passed, the flaming projections of his heart's fancy. Again he kissed them, and implored them to linger with him; and their coquettish smiles, once so near, and warm and yielding,

were now but an inch away. He chanted, he remembered
not how many anthems in honor of the dead, scores
of them, hundreds. And behind them, closing the
procession, Ariadne, –

"Ariadne, the babbling brook, offspring
Of the hoofed comrade of Pan,
Ariadne, the flower scented.
Drowned in my blood, suffused
In my substance, till death will sunder us. . . .
In the grove, in the grass, in the air,
In the sough of the wind that sings of her,
In the river-beds, in the eyes of the crickets!
And one day they took her away from me –
Never to be seen again. . . ."

"Devil!" he screamed. "Imp, crook, and elf,
Beelzebub's disciple!"

"I am nothing of the kind," Atma calmly said. "I am
just an ordinary magician with common sense, not worse
than Duroff. I presume you heard of that great creator of
illusions? Of course, art can get along without common
sense. You, fed on clefs and flats, ought to know better
than that. Well, let's go, our journey is long."

"I shan't budge!" he howled. "Even if your father,
Lucifer, and mother, Astarte, with their son, Petronius,
your own brother, club me to death. Here I shall crouch

in the road, and maybe Ariadne will appear in the dusk of the illusory night."

Atma whispered: "You are childish. You wish to create illusions upon illusions, and illusions of illusions, as if life itself were not sufficient for you. You are striving at all cost to disrupt the wonderful harmony of relativity which alone can harmonize and co-ordinate the endless iridescent reverberations of phantoms of things that perhaps once were."

"I won't go. I am staying right here! I am not afraid of you," he stubbornly resisted.

"Fool that you are," the other said, puzzled by his stubbornness. "Know then that all that centaur business was nothing but a vision, a monstrous unreality I had created for you, to relieve the monotony of our trampings!"

"Ariadne! Ariadne! The foam-begotten Aphrodite, the rainbowy bubble!" He wept noiselessly.

"Don't you understand that no centaurs exist in our days? Where have you seen such ridiculous creatures, except in textbooks of mythology? You, simpleton."

"A joke, a hoax!" he exclaimed. "But the reality of her embrace. The seething heat of her kiss!"

"No more real than the erotic incubus that agitates the breast of a young boy late at night, almost at dawn . . . and makes him lose himself in amorous trepidations and give himself to a nonexistent woman. Thus a man marries a dream."

"Thus I married a dream," he repeated, like an echo. "Of course, I don't believe you! I am not dreaming. And I never have dreamed. I shall seek Ariadne all over the continent, if I have to go to the North Pole. As soon as I have reached Murman I shall offer a reward to whoever finds my wife, my lover, my love, my heart, my burning torch!"

And he fell on the grass, and sobbed, and bit the grassblades, munching the salty jagged stalks. If it was a dream, God, why did he awake?

"What do you want now?" Atma asked.

"For the last time, show me Ariadne."

"Such feelings are unworthy of a man with great musical ability," Atma sighed rebukingly. "But I bow before your weakness, and I shall grant your wish, realizing the extent of your despair, just to show you how little you know of illusions."

He got up, and they began to march. Suddenly alongside of them the flimsy projection of Ariadne emerged, and brushed by and beckoned them. Swiftly she passed. He wondered if she recognized him. For a moment it seemed to him that her lovely oval face tilted sideways, and the glimmering eyes smiled at him.

"Ariadne! Ariadne!" he exclaimed.

The halo-brimmed oval of her face shone in the glimmer of her lucid smile.

"Ariadne! Eurydice!" he cried, stretching out his fingers. "Stay! Stay! . . . Why do you merge with the air so swiftly, so cruelly, so irretrievably!"

His body rose and floated up to her. An inch divided them. Her shadow seemed to be throbbing with faint memories. Hardly knowing what he was doing, almost against his will, he began to sing *Blue Lagoon*, at first softly, then louder and louder, rousing the entire valley. Orpheus had thus bewailed the vanishing shadow of Eurydice.

Dawn unfolded slowly and the tremulous outline of Ariadne vanished. His song turned into a sob. He wept bitterly. A flood of tears seared his lids and forced them open. Only then did it occur to him that all the time he had spoken and bickered and sung, his eyes were closed, and the vision of Ariadne had burned its way through his eyelids.

Families of parrots sat on lower branches, and ingratiatingly peeped at him, their cowled heads cocked, as if they still heard the vanished strains. In the wan azure of morning their purple hoods were tinted a fairy pink. Charming little apes had scuttled down from tree-tops, forgetting their enmities, and listening, long hands clasped on their hairless bellies. Near him, touching his feet, were numberless squirrels, nuts in their hands, rigid, oblivious of food in their admiration. At a distance, he saw snakes crawling toward him, their heads gracefully lifted and rhythmically moving in pleasurable wonderment.

"Wait," he said. "Let me catch . . . my breath. . . . But at last we are in Arkhangel . . . What a dreary-looking place!"

They reached the top of the rock on which dilapidated huts were pasted, drab sentinels of a wealth of pagoda-shaped buildings high upon the hills. As they passed the huts, Ariadne reappeared and vanished for ever.

"Ariadne!" he cried. "The hot boiled pitch in my veins that has created you! The incarnation of all my suppressed desires leashed by drab necessities! I counted the embraces, I felt the inferno of your thighs. Where, O where, will I find another you? Through what transformations can I reconstruct your vanished form? Into what did you lovely contours melt? Soft as the air itself, your lines hovered before my eyes. I trembled, I burned in benumbing vigils. Have I not carried you on my shoulders in the devilish flight on the meadow, to the rhythmic *cri-cri* of the grasshoppers? Have I not lost my sense, like a young girl who scorns clothing? The frogs were rehearsing their musical continuities, the moon silvered the crests of blue ripples, and you lay beside me, on your back, looking into the starry sky. Shadow of a shadow of candlelight.

"Dreams have no coherence and love-adventures are like dreams. But Ariadne, Ariadne, once more press your frigid limbs against the vanishing intensity of my anguish! Now all sings in me, and the throes of creation shake my frame. Ariadne, naked Diana, centaur-child of the tipsy anthropoid, sister of Pan's godson! . . . Should you beget a son, a child of Chimera, Chimera himself, will you ever come to me in a dream, and nod your lovely head with a recognizing smile? For I shall live only for you, and through you. Widowed, and orphaned now, in what sounding spheres does your velvety body bathe?"

The languorous sounds of horns reach his ears. The village is all agog with mirth. The fair has started, and they are hastily climbing uphill.

They are about to enter Arkhangel.

"Now we have reached Arkhangel," he said, or wanted to say, as he opened his eyes.

He was in a small room smelling of stale fish and beer. From somewhere came the raucous sounds of a hurdy-gurdy, whiningly wavering in fits of coughing and stuttering. The song was unrecognisable, as if the hurdy-gurdy had the whooping cough and bemoaned the cruelty of the artist who made her work.

"Where was I?" he cried aloud to drown the arrogant voice of a certain red manikin. It did not occur to him then that his throat was dry of sounds. At the time, however, he was quite amazed that no one answered his loud clamoring.

There is no sensation comparable in sweetness to that immediately following the awakening from nightmare. The mind is on the borderline. The eyes are open, but the soul is still closed to the outward world and hearkens to the weird chords of fantastic melodies, defying recapture. The heated mind is cooling off, the body is strangely light, ready to rise and hover in inaccessible ethereal spaces. And yet, all the weight and substance of bodies are there,—and the consciousness of reality is slowly penetrating the mind.

After a while he began to realize that he was alive. Near him on a broken chair lay pickles, potato-rinds, dry fruit, stale bread, and a tin cup.

His first impulse was to reach for the cup. But his

arms were paralyzed. So helpless was he, that he began to weep. But even his tears were scant.

A woman entered and gave him a drink.

"I thought you were dead," she simply said. "We expected you to die yesterday, that's what the surgeon told us."

"I am not going to die," he roared with disgust.

"Gee, you can't even open your mouth," the woman said with a smile that cut her face in four parts. For a moment it seemed to him that her face was under her legs, and her feet above her head.

"Eat, eat!" he suddenly exclaimed. These were the first words he heard himself say. The power of speech had come back to him and he spoke feebly, whiningly, like an idiot.

"Who'll give you bread?" she laughed, and again her face fell under the floor. "You poor fool, there isn't much food here for the healthy ones. . . . However, we'll see what can be done."

In the evening she came again, and related to him the details of his death. It seemed that after having grown delirious and having threatened to strangle the girl, he had collapsed and remained unconscious for nine days.

"What girl?" he asked.

"You were here with a girl, and a Choovash, or Mordva, or some kind of Kalmuck," she said.

"Weren't you?"

His mind was disturbed. Weak as he was, he tried to raise his head. He recalled the details of his dream, a certain Ariadne, the centaur, Atma. With what painful lucidity these lovely creatures shone, beckoning him across the drab canvas of the Northern tavern!

"Ariadne!" he whispered. Then he recalled who she was.

"Ariadne, Ariadne!" he shouted. "How could I have forgotten your lovely shape?"

"Where is she, where is the girl?" he asked, trembling.

"Why, they left two days after you fell sick," the woman answered. "They paid me for one month, and asked me to take care of you, although they were pretty sure you wouldn't live more than a week or so. A lovely girl she was, though."

"Stop fooling me!" he angrily snapped. "When do you expect Ariadne back?"

"Eat your gruel first," she said, arranging his shabby blanket. "We'll talk later."

He fell asleep, and dreamt that he was slowly rising in an elevator to Ariadne's apartment. Just as he was about to ring the bell the door vanished and he awoke. His eyes were moist. Exhausted by the devilish revelry of dreams he sobbed helplessly.

Though fed on herring, bones, and gruel, he grew stronger and craftier. He knew that the buxom woman near his bed was keeping Ariadne away for some reason or other, perhaps intending to demand ransom. Whenever he turned the conversation upon Ariadne and Atma, she smiled and told him long stories that were simply monstrous. Because of the haste with which she switched to topics wholly unrelated to that uppermost in his mind, he knew that the wicked woman was hiding something from him. He strained his eyes to see better, but her face was drowned in a vast smile, and he had the impression one gets looking at a candle.

In a few days he was able to reconstruct the events leading to his delirium: there really was a girl named Ariadne, and Atma with her, as well as her father, the Centaur.

But here his thoughts were bungled. The centaur, at least, was undoubtedly part of the typhoid delirium, as also his little son who would so gently shove a lovely nose under his armpit. But Ariadne? And Atma?

He reached for the violin, but it fell out of his hands back on the pillow, and again he wept with chagrin. He still was very weak.

Once, when he felt strong enough to play a game of *durak* with the girl—he noticed that she was young and quite lovely, and that in many ways she suggested Neyla—he begged her to take him to Ariadne. With tears in his eyes he promised to love her if she would only bring back Ariadne.

She laughed, and blurted out: "Oh, stop kidding me . . . You think I am joking, huh? Don't you know she ran away with that Mordva, or whatever kind of Kalmuck he was?"

"When did it happen?" he asked.

"I told you a hundred times," she said impatiently. "You wouldn't listen to me . . . Well, she was no good anyhow."

"How do you know?" he asked.

"She palavered a whole night with one of the commissars, and got fine clothes and money. Next day she left for Moscow in a special car. That's the kind of girl you were stuck on."

"Keep quiet, you," he snapped.

A deathly terror seized his heart. He was calm, calmer than he thought he would be. Was it because he had lived through his entire life in those fifteen minutes of dreaming, and was wed to her, and bathed in the azure coolness of her nudity, and had grown mutely reconciled to the idea of losing her some day? It passed like a dream, and a dream it was, now confined to the abysmal depths of his subliminal self with so many other memories that had once been realities. Perhaps he realized that after the unaccountable bliss of those fifteen minutes, nothing mattered. Crowning that eternity, even death itself and the black spaces thereafter seemed cool and assuaging like the interior of a nymph's grotto dreamed about on a sultry day in Patras or Constantinople.

Several weeks after he recovered, Marfa took him out for a walk. When he put on his trousers, he discovered that all the jewels had been stolen. He showed no signs of amazement. He could never find them; they did not even belong to him. Nor was it safe to become entangled in such matters when one had a false passport. He could not banish the strange feeling that the accursed jewels would bring calamity to their possessors, as had already been the case for the negro, and the notary, and, no doubt, with Pakhom himself. It was Ariadne's turn.

When he returned to the tavern, refreshed by the long stroll in the autumnal afternoon, he seized his violin and kissed its smooth back—the priceless reality of what otherwise seemed like a visit to a non-existent region. Like a link with Ariadne was the instrument. Convalescing in the tavern steeped in herring odors and the stridencies of a hurdy-gurdy, he played scales, tremulous and false, accompanied by the whining of Marfa. As his hands grew stronger, she began to listen with vague surprise. Then she knelt before him, and begged him not to play, for she had grown dizzy from excessive sobbing, and her head was in a vortex of violently clashing waves and she saw things that made her tremble.

But his soul longed for communion with the one unearthly vision that had once entered his life, then had been so miraculously deflected to the opposite side of this globe, disappearing forever and leaving a row of harrowing images.

When Marfa came at night, and kissed and caressed him and begged for caresses, he kissed her, but remained silent and indifferent to her, and not even her tears could move him.

One day he left, never to return again, reached the border line, and invaded Arkhangel.

The Americans were good to him, and he played for them through all the long journey to New York.

H E was back in New York, ready to resume his life where he had left it off at the moment of his hasty flight to Russia. With time the whole Lidda episode acquired an almost symbolic significance. Because his mind refused to become reconciled to her sudden and irrevocable disappearance, he treated her as part of his typhoid delirium. And yet, though dead and unattainable, she warmed his life. He saw her stepping over roses, her tiny toes touching the petals caressingly, skipping the thorns with an intuitive scornful wisdom. From rose to rose, from bush to bush she hovered, until merged with the festivity of an esoteric Spring. Beyond her was—what? Into the gutters of the North, into the most abject of the wretched villages he had to stray to find her among midgets and hermaphrodites. In the dens of Galata, in the gruesome by-streets of old Marseilles, in the reeking city of Kharbin his feverish memories sought her, and delved through the porthole of despair into the turbulent sea of humanity in quest of her mocking vision. At times the desire to see her—if only in a dream—was so burning that like a despicable ham-actor he clutched at his temple and moaned: "Ariadne! Ariadne!" And the three visions slowly swam by, Ariadne, Lidda, and the daughter of the centaur, the dream of dreams, the very essence of his life.

In New York he was not completely forgotten, and Dr. Kreisel was the first to pay him a visit. Yashu was in

Chicago, and he wrote to him in a rather summary way about his harrowing experiences. Feofani was teaching at Peabody Institute, where Kazarinoff's fame had found a place for him. Neyla had disappeared tracelessly. Outside of these he knew no one.

He had to use all the persistency of despair to avoid being exhibited by Dr. Kreisel, who lionized him. He did not want to see anybody while he was completing his Centaur's Daughter, for he listened to voices utterly incompatible with the screechy noises around him. As a discordant note came Ladislas Lerner's letter with a questionnaire for the Biographical Dictionary of Jewish Musicians, with an order blank for a ten-dollar copy or the twenty-dollar "handsomely bound in chamois,and inscribed by Ladislas Lerner, sometime the pupil of Rimski Korsakoff." And when Dr. Kreisel playfully informed him that Ariadne was back in the States and that now, after the death of the Count Rostovtsev, she might be more amenable to courtship, he lowered his head and stammered wildly and incoherently. He saw the shrivelled face of Berlioz and the bewildered figure of his actress basking in his glory. It is dangerous to cast a hypnotic spell over women and have them mistake adoration for love.

The bewildering year that drove a wedge into his life had all the magic coolness of a distant blue ridge faintly tinged with gold. He lingered with a helpless languor on his marriage to the Centaur's daughter. Of the three Ariadnes but this one had remained, faithful to him, even though vanished through sheer force of cosmic order. Out of that dream came the Centaur's Daughter, completely formed in his mind even when he had dreamt it, even as he had lain in the fish-smelling tavern at the gate of Arkhangel. The melodies he had elicited from the trees and the brook and each blade of grass so tenderly trembling, so eager to participate in the twilight rehearsal, still rang in his tingling ears like the quivering echo of crystalware.

He wrote slowly, without haste, for the memory of those fifteen minutes was unforgettable: he was merely transcribing the inexorable dictation of Nature. Now and then this or that heartrending episode stood out in bold relief, and his hand quivered and he closed his eyes. He was now the bearer of one divine dream that cast a lunar softness over all his yearnings. Tears trembled in his eyes as he wrote with a sudden pang of eternal hunger. He must transmit his dream to the world and forever quicken its pulse. It was now strangely immaterial whether Ariadne—any one of the three— would hearken to these strains. He was slowly reaching immortality in his attitude toward death and life. After the Centaur's Daughter had been completed he would die? Slowly and relentlessly the conviction grew within him. It would be a beautiful and majestic death. He saw himself in the Northern forest, like Beethoven blindly groping his way in the storm. The wind played in the hollows of the trees as if the forest were a huge organ. The snow fell over him and muffled the symphony of the wind with a warm breath of dying memories. Suddenly all was transformed into an exotic tropical lagoon hot with drowsy sunset, and he frantically swam toward Ariadne floating in the distance, the pall of her silky golden hair like a net spreading over the glimmering surface. The chorus of the Centaur's daughters sang:

My name is Aruana,
My tail's aglitter.
In blessed Nirvana
Our days we fritter.
Midsummer cobweb,
Gossamer dreams,
World's illusion
Is just what it seems.

As if subduing the invisible orchestra, he waved his hand, dismissing the huge cathedral in which he saw himself dying to the blissful strains of the Centaur's Daughter sung by a chorus of white women in a dreamy ecstasy of reminiscences of their former lives on earth. The last chords were vanishing under the cupola and he breathed for the last time, as if his soul consisted on nothing but that melodic exuberance which he had just given up. Somewhere there was Pakhom, and the Tsarevich, and the village full of derelicts, and there were probably millions full of these. Around him, bending over him, stood Parrel, Eiler, Feofani, Kazarinoff, and Ladislas Lerner, and they all seemed the manifestation of the same Infinite power, and it was he who had been born to reconcile all as a dream dreamt by a superior being in a moment of playful abandon. If life was a dream, what was art? The memory of a dream. And the memory is so much more poignantly lingering than the thing itself; for the true immortality of being is in the memory of it.

H E conducted the Centaur's Daughter at one of the regular Philharmonic concerts and the Brahms Association supplied the pagan chorus. The leader of the Club, a pupil of Max Bruch and Humperdink, frothed at the mouth and swore in German at the inability of the chorus to get on to the unusual tonalities, and at the tonalities themselves that puzzled his Club.

Nevertheless, the Symphonic Poem was received enthusiastically. There was unmistakably a strange genius, morbid and froward, yet powerful, typically American in his exuberant pagan vitality, some maintained; typically international in his exuberant vitality, others said; typically and prophetically Hebrew in his exuberant vitality, Ladislas Lerner claimed in his exclusive article in The Jewish Sentinel, though his heart ached as he wrote the eulogy, for somehow he felt that for once he was face to face with a great man. But The Jewish Sentinel would publish none but laudatory articles; if a Jew is to be panned, why speak of him at all?

And women, who, as a rule, will try anything once, found him exceedingly intriguing and sought exclusive possession through morning mail.

He felt her presence in the audience, and as he wormed his way through the rows of applauding musicians, he did not let his eyes wander to the first row where he had before seen Yashu and Feofani, now sober and dry and taciturn. His heart beat with such violence that again he thought he was about to die. And because of the certainty of his imminent death, he flung himself into the very thick of his last creation, eager to evoke for his own self the rasp cri-cri of the grasshoppers on the shore near the grotto, the nuptial gift of his father-in-law the centaur. The song of Aruana, the goldfish caught in the net of Ariadne's hair, rose with the pathos of a Delphic choral, intermingling with the powerful strains of the magnificent orchestra. The unbelievable sweetness of that one life within a life brought tears to his eyes, and he rose on his toes in a faint memory of his ancient nomadic flights, ready to float in the endless azure and merge forever with the cosmic harmony, the unity with which he now felt with hitherto unexperienced poignancy.

In the dressing room he gave vent to his despair. Completely exhausted, he fell into a chair and covered his face with his hands still trembling as if they were holding the baton. Crushed under the weight of his imaginary death, he failed to recognize Feofani, black and dignified and reassuring, and Yashu, who, stern with the responsibility of the sudden success, helped him to gain control over himself,

He opened his eyes. His heart beat alarmingly, but he was alive. Then the door opened, and Ariadne entered, accompanied by the inevitable Dr. Kreisel and a splendid looking young man of the Spanish type,—the same satyr and a different faun. It was the real Ariadne, stripped of her dreamy appurtenances, but as beautiful, even though with a strange glimmer of irony and deceit in her eyes.

He quickly rose with the jerky movement of a puppet. He was very calm, hardly understanding the significance of her visit.

"I believe" . . . Dr. Kreisel said with slight embarrassment. Ariadne stretched out her arm with her usual languorousness and let him kiss her hand.

"I understand you have just returned from Russia," she said, seemingly amazed at his aloofness. "You must have had a hectic time form what I have read in the papers."

"What papers?" he exclaimed, puzzled.

"I'm to blame," Yashu apologized. "I expanded your letter into an article and the World took it."

"Excellent press-agent stuff," Dr. Kreisel commented, eyeing Vladi with intense curiosity, intent on making the best of his association with this somber genius and at least having him autograph the manuscript of the Centaur's Daughter, or give lessons in counterpoint to Mme. Kreisel. He noisily invited all those present to celebrate "the historical event in American music and art" by tasting the new shipment of caviar and Martel.

"However," he turned to the Spaniard, "you must not

be jealous, and let the genius have at least half an hour with our Ariadne. . . . By the way: this is Señor Alonso Rivera y Molinas . . .”

Diplomatically he dismissed his car and hailed cabs. At last they were alone.

“We were in Russia together,” she said dreamily. She had not changed in the least. She was as beautiful and as intriguing, but it seemed a cheap sort of intrigue. “How vexing that you could not find me there!”

The sudden swerve of the cab threw her into his arms, and his hands clasped behind her warm and resilient body. She did not seek to release her body.

“And I was just—just about to begin to find interest in you,” she whispered.

He slowly released his hands and wiped his face. The sudden contact with her body brought to his mind the flaming scenes in the grotto and her little impish brother. A wistful smile hovered over his face. She would not understand.

“Do you remember that last night?” she suddenly asked and leaned against him. “In all the love and worship that surround me I shall be looking forward to you and your genius. Alonso simply idolizes me, but—*por Dios!*—outside of his strength, height, mustache, and wealth, there is nothing in him that can compare with you.”

He kept on staring at her with a sudden hatred. Even

as she had once picked up a few words of Russian, thus now she lapsed into charmingly and wilfully distorted Spanish, lisping the words delightfully. She was the symbol of the adaptable female, as low in the order of the universe as certain types of gipsies. Her eyes still had the depth of sapphires, but there was a void there; her voice still possessed the modulations that suddenly transform the lukewarm purrings of a string quartette into a passionate outburst, but the basic tonality itself was false and shallow.

He suddenly caught a faint vestige of the Count's smile in her own. She still affected certain ways of one of her lovers. With a sudden fraternal pity—the feeling of unity with all males, alive and dead—he remarked, breathing heavily:

"He certainly is no match for the late Count."

She grew pale and laid her hand on his.

"Did you see him in Russia?" she whispered.

"I witnessed his death," he lied. "It was a tragic, an unforgettable scene."

"Oh, how I loved him, how I loved him, and how unhappy I am now," she cried, and her shoulders convulsed. Tears welled in her eyes, now huge and scared, doubled in size by the magic lucency of her sparkling tears. She bit her laced handkerchief, but her trembling chin would not be steadied, and finally she flung her head on his chest and sobbed helplessly.

"Don't cry, Ariadne," he said simply, stroking her head. "I too lost a shadow."

"He was noble and strong," she stammered between sobs. "And torn—torn to pieces. . . . Oh, the memories of his embrace and ecstasy of passion! As if it had never happened. . . ."

"Forget him," he said, wiping her tears. "And forgive me, for I don't think I am in a mood to face light and people to-night. I am leaving you now."

Her eyes were dry and narrowed.

The cabs stopped and he respectfully led her out and, as if afraid of being pursued, took quick leave of the group. Feofani and Yashu followed him in a hasty retreat.

"He still loves me," Ariadne whispered to Dr. Kreisel as they were entering the foyer of the latter's house.

They returned to his room. Yashu was drunk with happiness, and now and then lapsed into gipsy jargon. Suddenly he fumbled in his pocket and produced a telegram slip.

"I received this before the concert, but I didn't want to bother you," he said. "You can never tell. Maybe it's bad news. Now you can read it."

He opened the telegram and read and reread the incredible lines: "Coming tomorrow Wednesday liner Paris Lidda Ariadne."

THE boat arrived late in the afternoon. It had been raining during the day, but toward evening the sky was clear.

The sudden appearance of Ariadne had left a faint promise of message from another dear departed one. And now that Lidda was near, he hearkened with a blissful serenity to all the shadows of his past. Fragments of passionate whisperings, details of trysts came to his memory, and the merging visions of the three Ariadnes—inalienable, unseverable—were blended in the devilish rush of days and years. How strangely she was coming back—the departed one, the one who had vanished from the silvery screen of earthly projections and dropped into Lethe! And thus others will reappear regardless of whether they shall be seen or not, whether it be our good fortune to regale our hearts with a hurried glance at a casual meeting in the short course of our zigzag wanderings, and steal another handshake, another smile, or once more press body to body as if they were still aquiver with earthly yearnings and burning desire, and not reduced to ashes and dust!

Porters brushed by, bells clanked, a negro yelled lustily and unintelligibly. Milling crowds surged endlessly in the huge shed and he, knocked about, stared at the yawning fissures of doors and windows. How she must have changed, he thought, how he himself had changed since they had parted, seemingly forever, in the seething turmoil of the first outbreak of the revolution!

The crowd thinned, the whistles and yells grew less shrill. Footsteps echoed pleasantly and unobtrusively. Where was she? He was chilly with expectation. The horizon became purple in the anticipation of a glorious sunset, but he still trembled with cold. All the scenes in the village, the grotto, the Feofani-looking centaur, the woman in the tavern with the face of Neyla, the blind men and the dreadful thumping of their sticks,— all these sped through his memory with a deadening swiftness, leaving a gripping sadness, a morbid sense of irrevocability in their wake. Frigid with benumbing reflections, he stood near the gangplank, taking in the undulating crowd with unseeing eyes.

"Here, Vladi," a tremulous, sobbing, hysterical voice called. She tugged at his sleeve. How familiar, how strangely familiar her pale face was, her almond shaped eyes, the graceful oval, so noble, so chaste. . . . Her eyes drew close to him, her cheeks sought his, and he bent toward her, hypnotized. And suddenly the realization that he was at the end of his quest came to him, and he burst forth in a wild cry:

"Ariadne! Lidda . . . You!"

She fell into his arms, unable to restrain herself, unwilling to believe that it was he, recalling the day she had stolen out of the vast crackling forest and brought him—the dead one—on a faithful Ural mare to the first village. Wiping her cheeks, unable to repress his own tears, he stroked her head, and spoke to her as he had once spoken to her in that accursed village and the somber prison yard, as if nothing had changed, as if she had left him but yesterday. Through his tear-dimmed eyelashes he could see her beloved face, as strangely disturbing as it was on the meadow near the lake where her father, the centaur, squabbled with his refractory wife.

Men and women passed by, porters brushed them aside and cursed, yet they stood there, prey to one and self-same emotion. Down from the limitless sky she had come, from behind the huge trees susurrating in the evening breeze. With a sudden clarity he saw her little brother, so playful, so irresistibly frolicsome. Their tears mingled and rolled down to the lips. Unmindful of the briny drops, they looked into each other's eyes. He recalled the first Ariadne and the pathetic fallacy of his illusions. Yet how beautiful those illusions were! What warmth, what glow they had infused into his life, into his heart, what fantastic play they had brought into his solitary ecstasies! The very natures of men and women are polar. The only blissfully near, so delightfully understandable woman he had ever known was the Ariadne of his dream, the daughter of the centaur, the one that had crumbled to dust as soon as he awoke, even as Shankara had said: that the circling world is like a dream, crowded with desires and hates, and that in its own time it shines as real, but on awakening becomes unreal.

He glanced aslant at Lidda. Sunset purple tinged her heavy tresses with gold and opal. A saintly nimbus framed her oval face. She strained his face to hers. Why were his eyes so cold, so hostile? Was she like first, or like second Ariadne? How beautiful are the illusions woven around one's illusions about a woman! . . .

With a sudden warmth he answered her passionate kiss. He now definitely felt that he loved her, and that around no other woman would he so willingly weave the musical gossamer of his visions. "Where is your kerchief?" he exclaimed teasingly. "And the homespun blouse and the thick burlap skirt and hemp sandals? Where are your midgets? How beautiful you are, how unbelievably more beautiful since I saw you last. . . ."

He clung to her arm, as if afraid that she would suddenly turn into a shadow and merge with the grey walls behind her. She was the only link with his past; she was his present, his past, his future. Around her were woven the cobwebs of uncertainties, dreams and realities. The fugitive moments of tardy hours and days of life were surcharged with disturbing lingering tangibility now that she was with him again. Her imprint was on everything, and even the dead asphalt exhaled grotesquely shaped vapors under her steps.

Dazed, he followed the porter. Perhaps from behind the lamppost he would step out, her impish brother, stroking his tousled curls, even as she had stepped off the warm pulsating boat and transformed a dream into an exotic reality. . . . The main thing was not to walk too fast, and linger, linger in this mad onrush of strangling waves, to stare into quickly dashing faces and to absorb the kaleidoscope of life. . . .

"But you hadn't hated me these days?" she asked ingratiatingly, as the cab drove up to the fifties. "I had thought . . . you were about to . . . die. And they were after me. I forgot their names."

"No, I never hated you. . . . Except in that dream."

"What dream?"

"Life is a dream," he said, "and love is a dream within a dream, and there is awakening within awakening."

"Let us dream together," she whispered with agony. "I do not know why you torture me, but I love you more than ever. More than when you were about to die. . . . I was all alone in that forest. Soon Atma arrived, and we carried you into the tavern. When we lost all hope, I took the diamonds and ran off with Atma to the border. Half of the jewelry went to bribe the guards."

And Atma was killed, she added. This time for good, and buried on a hill to the music of the wind. He was killed by the enraged peasants from whom he had stolen a horse to join her.

Stumbling in the maze of dreams and realities, tottering over the debris of past visions, his mind slowly—yet how reluctantly—disentangled the mess of disjointed figures, distorted faces, unbelievable landscapes. In the hotel, incredulously kissing her body, he asked what had happened to her brother. What brother? Now, did she not have a brother, who used to shower him with an icy torrent every morning as they awoke in their grotto? She smiled.

Swept by the avalanche of reminiscences, he spoke feverishly and with the eloquence of despair about his dream. Would she understand him? He told her that all these days he had lived on the glow instilled in him by the breath of Ariadne—her breath. The despair of separation, the pathos of never seeing her again was allayed by the elemental warmth with which she had enveloped him. Nothing could equal the serene happiness pervading his heart at the mere thought that some day he might see her again, even if at the end of his long journey. It was as though she were playing a childish trick on him and hid in the bushes. Often he dreamt of her. But as time went on, the dreams grew less morbid. Her caresses still lingered on his skin, and her rough kittenish tongue tickled his nose, and he cried in his sleep and murmured Ari—ad—ne. . . . And then came a day when she disturbed him no longer. He knew she was basking in the sun in a far-off meadow bordered by graceful pines. Her elderly parents would take care of her. Her wondrous little brother must have grown to manhood—the centaurs grow fast—and carried her on his shoulders in their eternal nomadic flights.

In the dim twilight thousands of faces beckoned them. They wanted no light. The visions glistened in their gorgeous coloring with all the tangibility of delightful dreams. Ariadne swept by like a panting dryad on the back of a mad centaur. And he wept over the spectral magic of Cyril Scott's Lotus Land, as she slowly sang it to him between kisses.

In the adjoining room Yashu played on his violaxophiano. The day was near when people would draw music out of the air simply by raising their hands and regulating the position of their knuckles. There would be no artists and no listeners, for the whole world would be one huge cathedral where day and night divine chorals would resound. With stirring candor the gipsy played . . .

Do not blame me, my beloved,
For my hopeless love of you. . . .

Slowly she steered his wavering mind through the jungle of memories. The centaur was a myth. Atma partly so. And the grim yard of the Inquisition? That was real. Pakhom, the cauldron, the chase, the blind men, the tavern, the Tsarevich. Yes, the Tsarevich. . . . And then, the nymph. . . . The nymph was a dream. And she had no brother.

A whole night they lay, greedily intertwining their memories. With tremulous fingers they lightly touched this or that dream, and went on. He thought of Ariadne, the dream that he had touched and turned into burning reality. Of the nymph who had merged with Ariadne, and played havoc with his perceptions and illusions. Of Lidda, the dream of a dream, twin of Ariadne, the centaur's daughter. Of his parents, shot and dissipated into oblivion. . . . Of all the shadows of the world, swift, palpable, that once were, and will be forever. And of all the shadows of shadows. And of Ariadne herself, the one, the Trinity-bearer.

And as he kissed her, nearly smothering her in the embrace that had been longing for her all these years, he embraced and merged with all of them.

www.ingramcontent.com/pod-product-compliance
Lightning Source LLC
Chambersburg PA
CBHW021321190726
48288CB00003B/910